I KNOW YOU'RE THERE

SUSAN ALLISON-DEAN

To Susan,
Mothers are
Special.
Warm Regards.
Sue Allison-Dean

Published by Sea and Farm
Cover by Deborah of Tugboat Design
www.tugboatdesign.com

ISBN 978-0-578-12141-3

Acknowledgements

Veering off my everyday path to write this first novel has felt a lot less scary and uncertain thanks to the immense support from my cheerleaders. There have been many, but special thanks goes to: The Johnson/Petrarca Family: Delores, Heidi, Felix and Julia; Diana Lynn Schaible, Terry Giacomo, Sara Smith and Amy Lingg. Thank you, John Dean for your valuable proofreading. To my editor and writing coach, Alice Osborn, the writers' version of Jillian Michaels, you've made me dig to write my best. Words cannot express my gratitude for all you have taught and shared with me, Alice. What would a book be without a cover? Deborah Sletten, thank you for your patience and graphic talent. To my bulldog, Bubba, thank you for making me get up every couple of hours to get some exercise during my writing. Last, but certainly not least, love and huge hug to my husband, Robert. Thank you for paddling the ship so I could write and keeping me focused.

In Memory of My Mother
Mary Lou Allison

Chapter 1

HELEN

OCTOBER 22, 1995

I woke up screaming, "It's my fault! Jill, it's my fault!"

Startled, I sat up and got my bearings. The top half of my white flannel nightgown was drenched in warm sweat that was now starting to cool. The alarm clock glared 12:20 am.

Thank God, I told myself. My daughter, Jill, a nurse at our local hospital had told me she was working a day shift, so she would be home in bed now. In my nightmare, Jill was in a room with two patients who both died at the same time. Frantic, she was screaming at them, "No, no, you can't die!! No, you have to wake up! They will blame me, they will say it is all my fault!"

Guilt eroded my stomach. Somehow I would need to tell my baby the truth.

Chapter 2

JILL

OCTOBER 23, 1995

The nurse was not going to wipe my face again, although I wished she would. Now she was lifting my right arm and it hurt. What the hell am I doing here, I wanted to scream!

"How is she doing today?" a male voice questioned.

"Her vitals have stabilized. She still hasn't regained consciousness," my nurse's gentle voice replied.

"Maybe that is a good thing for now. There's going to be a lot for her to handle. I'm glad that I'm not going to be the one to have to tell her." The male's voice got closer and I felt my chest being exposed and something cold walking along it, probably a stethoscope. Brut, I recognized that smell. My first boyfriend in high school wore that. This must be an intern; an attending doctor would wear something more expensive.

"Tell her what?" my head shouted to no avail.

"Her lungs sound clearer today, that's a relief. I didn't want to have to put her back on the ventilator," my chest was covered back up and his voice moved away. "If anything changes, please page me. I left my beeper number on the front of her chart."

"I will," my nurse replied. She hummed and gently lifted my other arm to wash it. The goose bumps were only temporary; she did a good job drying it off quickly. A twang of guilt hit me as I thought about how sometimes I was forced to rush through my elderly patient's bed baths. What was I supposed to do? Sometimes we were so short staffed.

The familiar sound of a curtain being drawn back followed with a female voice asking, "Jill's family is here, can I let them in?"

"Yes, they can come in for a short visit. I'm in the middle of getting her washed up." My nurse replied.

The curtain screeched closed again, then silence, then it screeched open again.

"Good morning," my nurse said trying to instill cheer in an otherwise tense, somber atmosphere.

"Good morning," I heard my father say, cautiously, from what sounded like the foot of my bed. I then felt warm hands surround my left hand.

"How is she today?" my mother asked quietly. She must be holding my hand, as the voice came from that direction.

"One of the doctors was just in. Her lungs are doing much better, that is a good sign," my nurse said hopefully. She left out the fact that I had not yet regained consciousness.

"When will she wake up?" my brother was here too.

"That's the golden question, we are hoping soon," my nurse informed them. "Why don't I give you a few minutes with her, then I will be back to finish up her bed bath." Silence once again filled the room, followed by the curtain screeching back and forth, then silence. This remaining silence was not empty; I could feel my family's presence and their worry.

My dad's hand swept my hair back and I could smell his scent come closer until he kissed me gently on my forehead.

My brother shouted a, "Hey, sis, we're here, we need you to get better, OK?" from the lower part of the bed and I felt a gentle tap on my leg. The sound of my younger brother, the jokester in the family, getting choked up was killing me.

Please, God, no, don't let me die. Please don't make my family go through that again. I begged with my mind.

Clearly at a lack for words, my family just stayed near my bedside, each in their own thoughts as the ICU monitors blinked away. The sound of the curtain screeching was a welcome relief to the overwhelming sadness in the room.

"Do you have any questions?" my nurse, the pillar of strength in this situation, asked.

"Is she in pain?" my mother asked.

"So far her vitals have been stable. Usually when people are in pain and can't communicate to us, we will see their heart rate and blood pressure go up. When that happens, we make sure to medicate them so they are comfortable."

"We're going to go to the cafeteria to get some breakfast so you can finish up what you were doing here," my father's voice insinuated he needed a break. "Then we'll be outside in the waiting area."

"That sounds like a good idea," my nurse replied. Her voice reflected experience and this in a small way made me feel a little better. "It is important that you all take very good care of yourselves now, too. We have things covered in here."

Another kiss on the forehead, this time one from each side of the bed and a sibling tap on the leg from my brother and then they were gone.

"OK, you ready for me?" A vibrant, loud voice

entered the room.

"Perfect timing," my nurse said. "Let's turn her towards you first and I'll wash her back."

Oh no, they were going to turn me. If my arm hurt as bad as it did when she lifted it, what was it going to be like rolling onto it?

I felt them tug me to one side, then two hands, the first placed behind my right shoulder and the other behind my right hip, and they rolled me like a log. The pain in my right arm was NOTHING compared to the screaming pain shooting through my right leg!

"OK, OK, we hear you," my nurse responded. "Her heart rate is shooting up. We better give her some morphine first."

"I'll wash her legs while you get the morphine." My nurse's helper gently righted me. "What a mess. Has anyone from her unit come to visit yet?"

"Yeah, two of the staff from her unit at Riverview Hospital did last night. I heard that they just stood by her bedside with tears coming out of their eyes. I think they are going to try to limit visitors for now to just family."

As I lay there, waiting to be injected with morphine, I desperately scanned my memory, trying to figure out why and how I got here. I recalled transferring a total hip replacement patient from the OR stretcher to her bed then leaning over and attaching her Foley bag to the bed so her urine would drain properly.

"This will help make it easier," I heard faintly. Within seconds every muscle in my body let go and the memory was gone.

BEFORE

Chapter 3

JILL
OCTOBER 14, 1995

"Are you going to Natasha's wedding?" Becky asked me as we walked down the hall together to help her patient get back into bed.

"To be honest with you, I want to. I like Natasha a lot, but yikes, how many weddings can I go to in one year?" I whispered as I pulled a pair of medium sized latex gloves out of the box on the wall, handed a pair to Becky and donned a pair on myself.

"I'm glad to hear you say that, "Becky whispered. "Don't get me wrong, it is really nice to get invited to our colleagues' weddings, but it's really getting expensive!"

Becky and I had a unique bond. The majority of our adult medical-surgical unit was staffed by mostly young, twenty something-year-old nurses, who in their off time were busy planning weddings. The group of us younger nurses filled most of the day and evening shifts, while our most senior nurses preferred to work the night shift. Becky and I seemed to be the only ones of the young crowd without sparkling diamonds on our left hands.

Becky was from the south, some small town in North Carolina. She originally came to our unit as a traveling nurse. To help ease the pressures of the nursing shortage, the hospital paid top dollars for nurses to come to our hospital and do rotations, usually for four months, during peak need times. Becky liked our unit a lot and our nurse manager liked Becky, so Becky decided to stay on full-time.

Becky was Rebecca Ann for short. Her hair was lighter blond than mine and straight. We would joke often about wishing we had each other's hair.

"Dang," she'd say with her southern drawl. "I'd much rather have your curls. Just wash, shake, and go! Do you know what a pain it is to blow dry my hair every morning? And if it is humid out, it just turns to frizz."

Becky knocked on Mrs. Swanson's door and announced, "Sweetie, Jill here is going to help me get you back into bed."

Mrs. Swanson looked up at us relieved, "Good heavens, that's good to hear, I'm tired."

Mrs. Swanson sat in a chair by the windowsill. She had become one of our long-term patients, waiting for nursing home placement because she could no longer care for herself at home. We joked that we should put mailboxes outside these patient's rooms and have their mail forwarded here, because they could stay for months depending on their type of insurance. Mrs. Swanson's gray braided hair completely exposed her soft black skin. I envied how the African American women didn't show wrinkles. Becky had a soft spot for Mrs. Swanson. She reminded Becky of her southern roots.

Becky's stories from the south gave me a window into a world foreign from my own. She talked about helping her mama make biscuits and sweet tea, while her daddy grew cotton in the fields. I have to admit, I don't even know what a real cotton plant looks like, but I love my 100% cotton sweatshirts and sheets! She would have my mouth drooling when she shared how much she missed real BBQ, fresh pulled pork smothered with homemade sauce hot and tangy, not sweet, and a side of collards that had been stewed with a hambone for flavor. When her stories led her to a bout of homesickness, she'd smack on her southern smile and say, "Well, you don't want to hear all about that!"

Becky led the way and arranged Mrs. Swanson's gown for "liftoff" while I prepared the cleaning supplies and new diaper. Then we each slid an arm under Mrs. Swanson, her facing forward and us facing behind her. The plan was to lift Mrs. Swanson, and pivot her into a sitting position in the bed. I would then help steer her shoulders to the bed while Becky swung her legs up and in.

"OK, Sweetie, on the count of three, we're going in. One, two, three!"

As we lifted Mrs. Swanson to a standing position, her soiled diaper fell from her and stool splattered all over, including us. My white pants were covered and stool oozed into my white clogs. I shot a look at Becky from behind Mrs. Swanson and mouthed without a sound, "I am going to kill you."

Becky cringed and mouthed, "Sorry!"

"Sweetie, we're going to sit you back down for a moment," with that we sat her back into the chair, half on the diaper, unable to do anything else since Mrs. Swanson was easily 180 pounds of dead weight.

"I'm so sorry," Becky whispered as we wiped off at the sink and gathered more cleaning supplies for Mrs. Swanson. "The skin on her bottom is such a mess, she's had diarrhea for a couple days now. We spent all morning getting her cleaned up and then I put a thick layer of zinc oxide on her bottom. I thought if I just sat her on the diaper and didn't wrap her in it, her skin might heal faster. I forgot I didn't stick it closed."

It was all we could do not to laugh. Having a sense of dark humor kept us sane.

My boyfriend, Jack, didn't find it funny at all, however, when I got home.

***

"What happened to you? Why aren't you wearing your white uniform?" Jack asked as he lounged on the couch with the clicker in his hand. Yes, Jack is his name. And, yes, we got teased about that all the time.

"I got shit on at work, literally." I said as I took my coat off. "No matter how bad a day you have at your job, you can't say that," I thought I was being witty.

"You what? Jill, that's disgusting!" Jack sat straight up, his face scrunched. "I hope you threw out your uniform! Oh, God, please, go take a shower before you come near me. I hope the person who shit on you doesn't have AIDS."

After seeing Jack's reaction, I didn't dare tell him my uniform was in a plastic bag in my knapsack and that I had planned on washing it in our washing machine twice with a lot of bleach. I headed straight for the bathroom and shed the blue scrub outfit I had gotten on loan from the Operating Room.

We used to be so in love, high school sweethearts. We spent most of our time together. Everyone just assumed we'd get married, even our families. We were so compatible that we believed it too. While other high school couples couldn't withstand the test of separation during the college years, we were still together. Perhaps I got too comfortable in our relationship and just assumed he would always be there for me, support me knowing I was trying to help people.

As I looked in the mirror, tears began to well up in my eyes. The stress between Jack and I was palpable. I couldn't deny it any more. It had been building for about a year now. After we graduated from college we immediately moved in together and planned to get engaged. Jack wanted to save up enough money for what he called a proper engagement ring. I, on the other hand, would have said yes if he gave me a ring from a Cracker Jack box.

We were so excited that we could now be together forever and start a family. Jack wanted to have kids right away. I wasn't quite ready. There were so many exciting things to do, travel, go out at night, and I had begun to think about getting my master's degree after seeing how amazing the advanced practice nurses were at the hospital. Jack didn't want to hear any of that. He was traditional. He wanted a family and a wife who stayed home. His vision of my career was that I would become a school nurse when our kids became school age. Maybe I could do just a shift or two a week to keep my skills up to date in the meanwhile.

Jack was used to getting what he wanted. His thick, curly, dirty blond hair and charming smile, complete with dimple, enabled him to talk his needs into your thoughts until you embraced them too. Now, don't get me wrong, he is a great guy! He was the one who got us involved in the church's mission trips and serving meals on holidays at the homeless shelter. He is fit and disciplined about what type of food he eats. I loved watching him play football all during high school and when I could get to his games in college. Smart too. Graduated college with honors and immediately got a job in finance on Wall

Street. Yup, Jack was the whole package, or so I thought. The one thing he lacked, however, was patience. I didn't really see this until I began to have needs and dreams of my own.

I took an extra long hot shower and just let the tears flow down with the running water. Jack's reaction hurt. It wasn't just how he felt about my career and what it entailed. The pain blended with a reality that I was getting hardened to what everyday people couldn't or, didn't want to deal with. The shield us nurses have that enables us to do things others find disgusting is a necessary survival skill for the job. The public seems to think a nurse just needs to be a nice person who can fluff pillows, comfort patients and hand out medications. Not so.

I wrapped my head in a Teddy Bear-soft white towel and put my spa robe on, a gift from Jack when we spent a weekend at the Ritz Carlton in New York City last fall. Why couldn't I just be content with this life? Women would kill to be in this position.

Jack was still on our slipcover sofa flipping channels when I entered the living room. Without looking at me, he continued, "I thought you have diapers for patients, I still don't understand how you got shit on."

I sat down on the moss green velvet winged back chair my mother gave us. It didn't really match our style, but since we only planned on living in this apartment in Nyack temporarily until we got a house, we took it. It was actually comforting to have a bit of my old home in our new home.

"We do have diapers, but Becky had left the patient's diaper open hoping to get more air to the patient's skin because she has a bad rash. Becky just forgot that she didn't have it closed when we got the patient up. It happens, we get busy, there is a lot to remember." I said solemnly.

Jack turned and looked at me. The anger and frustration drained from his face. He must have noticed the redness in my eyes, that no matter how much I tried, I couldn't wash away. Jack turned the TV off.

"Jill, I'm sorry." He looked down at the standard beige wall to wall carpet. "It's just, sometimes, your work is more than I can handle."

There it was. Out in the open. The next move in what had become an arduous emotional chess match, rather than a loving, fun relationship, was in my hands.

"Jack," now I looked down at the carpet. "I have been thinking. You know I love you, but maybe we have hit the end of the line." I clenched my core abdominal muscles, desperately holding back the next flood of tears that was waiting to break out pending Jack's answer.

"Jill, you know that I love you too. But, I've been thinking the same thing."

With that, the gushing tears flowed; we held each other tight, wishing what we both now acknowledged wouldn't be true. We eventually fell asleep on that big cushy couch in each other's arms.

Chapter 4

JILL
OCTOBER 21, 1995

As I entered Mr. O'Reilly's room I paused to admire, well, envy really, his interaction with his wife. Mrs. O'Reilly came in early every morning, before official visiting hours, to help him shave and have breakfast with her husband. Their affection for each other was evident; she doted over him like he was a prized racehorse.

"Now, Mary," Mr. O'Reilly said to his wife, trying to be stern, "you really need to get going now, so you can get home before this thunderstorm rolls in that they are talking about." Mr. O'Reilly pointed to the TV hanging from the ceiling in the corner of his room. The weatherman showed a map of our area with patches of red zones warning us what Mother Nature had up her sleeve.

I paused at the door.

"I will be fine, don't you worry. Jill, here will keep me in line!" he turned and winked at me with a smile.

"It's a tough job, but I think I am up for it." I confirmed.

Mrs. O'Reilly gathered her hand knit sweater, black leather purse and headed for the door. "OK, Jill, keep him out of trouble, will you," she said in her Irish brogue as she smiled. "I will be back for supper. Hopefully, the storm will have passed by then."

Left alone with Mr. O'Reilly I asked him, "How long have you two been married?"

"It will be 49 blissful years!" he beamed. "The kids are planning a big 50th party for us over in Ireland on an old farm in the county where Mary and I were born. We are really looking forward to that."

Forty-nine years, blissful, no less. "Mr. O'Reilly, if you don't mind me asking, how did you know Mrs. O'Reilly was the one?"

Mr. O'Reilly gave me a knowing smile as he looked at me with his big blue eyes. "Well, Jill, I know all you gals are looking for a romantic, poetic story, but the truth is there were others I thought about, but Mary was the right girl at the right time for me. If I had to do it over again, I would marry Mary again in an instant!"

I disconnected Mr. O'Reilly's IV bag. He was through with all his IV antibiotics and could drink on his own so he no longer needed it. As I did so, I thought to myself, right person, at the right time. That answer resonated in me. Maybe that was it. Maybe, Jack was the right guy at the wrong time for me. That made sense. It was also a little scary. So, when would the right guy come and when would my right time be? Worse yet, will there be a right guy or in my case a right time?

While my mind swirled around this quagmire, Mr. O'Reilly was kind enough not to ask me any questions. He turned his attention to the TV and occasionally glanced out the window.

"Don't worry," I patted his arm, "she'll be OK. She's a tough lady!"

He looked at me his shoulders relaxed a bit.

Becky knocked at the door and popped her head in, "Jill, we are on first lunch, just letting you know."

"OK, thanks."

Since our day shift started at 7 am, we were usually eager to get lunch breaks started by 11am. We tried to get off the unit and down to the cafeteria so we could really get a break, but many times we were so busy we just gobbled something down in the nurse's conference room on the unit in 15 minutes or less. With an hour to get organized, I decided that today that I was going to get a real break. If I finished giving all my patients' their morning medications, got those who could walk out of bed , and called in a consultation for the social worker to see my patient in 734, I might actually get off the unit before the afternoon influx started.

***

Becky swirled fresh strawberries into her yogurt as I sat down across from her at the two top by the window. She always brought her lunch and it was always healthy. I wished I had more discipline with my diet. Once I saw all the choices on the cafeteria menu I usually lost my ability to pick something healthy as my taste buds chose what they wanted.

"So, how is it without Jack at your place?" Becky asked. When Jack and I split, he decided to move into Manhattan to be closer to his job. I didn't really want to pay all the rent on our current place myself, but I could swing it until I came up with another option, so I stayed.

"Good, so far. It's a whole new experience having my own place. I've never lived alone before. Have you?" I took a bite into today's special: meatloaf.

"No. Growing up, our house was always bustling with my three siblings, our church friends and the staff. I never lived away from home until I joined the traveling nurses and they set me up with my two roommates in our apartment. I feel really blessed to have been paired up with some nice gals."

I listened patiently, gently nodded then turned to gaze out the window. Riverview Hospital got its name because it was situated on the Hudson River, just a few miles down from New York City. It was an old community hospital with new wings attached to the original structure like a remodeled home. The flow didn't make sense, but that's the way the place evolved. The best part was the cafeteria, which had a magnificent view of the river.

"Do you miss him?" Becky asked gently.

"Honestly, yes, and no, if that makes sense," I paused to give the question more thought before continuing. "I mean sure, I've known Jack for so long, he's like a cozy slipper. Our parents seem more devastated than we are. My mom calls every day asking me if I've made the right decision saying, 'Guys like Jack don't come around often you know.'"

I took a sip of my Diet Coke, no ice. "At the same time, it's kind of freeing. I've been sharing with you how things were not going well for a while now. So, maybe you'll understand that it's like a big gray cloud has lifted and the sun is coming out!"

Becky slowly spooned her yogurt into her mouth and let me continue.

"I went to pick out a new comforter yesterday. The choice was all mine. I didn't have to stop to consider what Jack's favorite colors were. I chose a really flowery pattern with vibrant purple and yellow. Jack NEVER would have gone for that. Brown, beige, gray, boring, boring, boring!"

"Has he called?" Becky asked.

My heart pinched. "No, I have to admit my ego is pretty bruised about that. After almost five years together, we reminisced a bit, said our goodbyes, packed up our stuff, and went our separate ways."

I didn't want to continue this line of questioning and potentially end up crying in the middle of the cafeteria so I shifted the conversation. "What about you? What's going on in your love life?"

"Well, I finally decided that if I am going to stick around here, then I probably need to get out on the dating scene." Becky lifted her hands up as her eyes lit up.

"And…." I egged her on.

"Well, I signed up on that new internet dating site. You put information about yourself in there, and what you are looking for, and they match you up with potential dates. Guys can also contact you after they search the database or vice versa. There are some good guys on their list, but I haven't contacted any. Call me old fashioned, but I think the guy should ask me on a date." Becky added an affirmative nod.

"So, have any guys asked you out?" I was curious.

"Well, so far it's kind of the same experience as going to a bar. There is what I am looking for, then there is what is looking for me!" Becky laughed. "I got a message from a gruffy-looking fisherman out at sea, a geeky research guy with glasses and what seems like a fitness-obsessed bike rider who looks prettier than me."

I laughed along with Becky, while my mother's voice haunted me. What if Jack really was a catch and I just threw him back in the ocean?

"I'll keep you posted, it has only been a couple of days since I signed on to it," Becky said as she put her empty yogurt container into her brown paper lunch bag. "Maybe you should try it."

"No, I am definitely not ready to jump into a new relationship just yet. But, if you do actually go out with one of these guys, make sure you call me and tell me where you are going first. This isn't like a blind date where at least the person who set you up knows the person."

"That's not a bad idea, I appreciate your kindness." Becky responded. And I knew she did. As social and nice as Becky was, she was still new to the north and hadn't established real roots yet.

"Code 5, location 7 East, Code 5, location 7 East," the hospital intercom announced, clearly and distinctly.

Becky and I sprang out of our chairs and, immediately left the cafeteria, leaving our half eaten lunches behind. Someone was in cardiac arrest on our unit. It was all hands on deck!

We hustled to the elevator, which luckily was open, and squeezed ourselves in, much to the displeasure of the other people all ready in it. We rode in silence until we were released to the seventh floor.

"Good, you're back. It's Mrs. Swanson," one of the new graduate nurses shouted at us.

We ran down towards Mrs. Swanson's room. The red crash cart, that most "civilians" would mistake for a Sears and Roebuck toolbox was already outside Mrs. Swanson's room. Our nurse manager, Marie, was at the bedside along with the intern, respiratory therapist and Natasha who was covering for Becky while we were at lunch. A nurse from the ICU was administering chest compressions. The intern barked out orders, "100% O2, one amp of epinephrine, get the paddles out." Natasha looked at us with that knowing look. Mrs. Swanson wasn't going to make it. Only us nurses knew why Natasha knew that. The group completed the code exercise anyway, until the intern called the code after 20 minutes. "OK, everyone, thank you. Time of death, 11:42 am."

"Why didn't you page me?" Becky asked Natasha as the three of us stood around the now deceased Mrs. Swanson.

"I was going to," Natasha said and now looked down at our patient, who remarkably looked quite peaceful. "But, you know, I still don't want to believe it is true when I see him."

By him, Natasha meant the man dressed all in black including a black hat. Only Natasha could see him entering a room just before a patient would die. It was one of those nurse's secrets that we carefully divulged to one another after spending long nights, weekends and holidays together. We feared someone would rat us out and we'd be required to undergo a psychiatric consult. These were the days before alternative medicine became so popular.

My "gift" was the ability to feel deeply. Intuitive they would call it later. I could sense when something was wrong. I could feel a patient's pain if I walked by their room. So much so, that the only way to relieve it for me was to make sure the patient got the appropriate pain care. This made me a very good nurse, but it wasn't always good for me. The seasoned doctors knew the nurses who had special powers beyond the norm. They would even share with us, "I know when certain nurses call me to come see a patient because, 'something is just not right', I need to come running."

"I'm sorry," Natasha said as she left me with Becky to handle Mrs. Swanson's post-mortem care. We did so with dignity, mostly in silence. Becky wiped a tear from her face with her sleeve. I knew that she knew there was nothing to stop this one. When the man in black came, it was your time to go.

***

It was a long day and I was looking forward to going home as we prepared our reports to give to the second shift in the nurse's conference room.

"I need someone to stay for the evening shift; Barb called in sick." Marie leaned on the door entryway, rubbed the back of her neck, as she broke the news in a tone deeper than usual. This was the third time this month Barb called in sick.

"Can't nursing administration send us a float nurse?" Natasha moaned.

"No, the floats are already assigned."

We each looked anywhere but at our nurse manager. We were all tired. Mrs. Swanson's death, two new admissions from the ER, four fresh patients from the Operating Room, and one more coming, a fresh total hip replacement. It would be a busy evening monitoring all these new patients, getting to know them, getting them settled in. Not to mention the regular patients we had on what would now be a full unit. At least there would be no more patients to admit, but the evening would add visiting family members. Most of them required care and explanations sometimes more than the patients did.

The silence was unnerving. Marie just stood in the door, feet planted firmly, and waited for someone to volunteer. We knew she didn't want to do it, but she had no choice. An inner voice warned me, "Let someone else do it," but my mouth opened and the words came out, "OK, I'll stay."

AFTER

Chapter 5

JILL
OCTOBER 28, 1995

"Jill, let's start with what you remember," Dr. Sol, a middle-aged female psychiatrist asked me in a soft, gentle voice. A sliver of hair escaped from the bun tightly wound behind her head. Although it dangled gently near her right eye, she paid no attention to it. Her focus was on me.

I looked from her to my parents sitting on the opposite side of my hospital bed. Dad's usual golden complexion was stale and leathery with a hint of sun from the frequent golf he played. My dad gave me a nod, as if to say, "It's OK, answer the question, we're here." My mom looked like it was all she could do to keep her eyes open, and there was something else not quite right about her, but now was not the time to try and figure it out.

I looked back at Dr. Sol. She sat in the hospital chair on the right side of my bed, leaning slightly forward, silently, and patiently, waiting for my response.

I laid my head back on the pillow and closed my eyes. Everything was such a jumbled blur. Was it just two days ago that I first opened my eyes? I remember a burning, pinching sensation in my right arm. I remember trying to swat at it with my left arm, as if it were a fly, but my arm would only move a couple of inches. Feeling frustrated, I tried again, and again, something around my left wrist was keeping me from reaching my right arm. Getting angrier, I found myself opening my eyes to see what was holding me back. That's when I re-entered "this world," feeling as if I had just climbed out of a deep, dark cave from winter hibernation.

Wrist restraints, just like the ones that we used on our unit to prevent confused elderly patients from pulling at their IV's and Foley bags, were wrapped snuggly around my wrists. A nurse wearing pale pink scrubs was trying to poke a needle into my right antecubital to get a blood sample. She looked up, surprised to see I was struggling. Her jaw dropped, when she saw my eyes open.

"Well, welcome back!" she gleefully cheered as she put down her needle weapon.

I looked at her blankly as I tried to figure out where exactly I was. An ICU, that much I could figure out quickly with all the monitors and the specialized air mattress bed I lay on.

My nurse jumped up and hit my call bell button, "Can someone please page Dr. Stanley, Jill just woke up!" she sang joyfully. "Do you know where you are?" she looked at me and held my right hand, abandoning her work on my arm.

I looked at her and made a lame attempt to say something but my mouth was so dry, it felt like cracked soil that had been baking in blazing summer sun with no water for weeks. The only sound that came out was something that sounded like, "Eehh."

Sizing up the situation quickly, as only an experienced nurse would, the nurse in pink coached me to relax, "Try not to talk yet," while she gathered oral care supplies. Before I could object, she was wiping my mouth with sponge tipped lollipops soaked in lemon oil. "You poor thing, your mouth must be so dry." I gagged from the collection of fluid gathering in the back of my throat and the accidental swabbing of my esophageal opening. Again I tried to yank out of the wrist restraints. "As soon as the doctor gets here we'll ask for an order to take those off," the nurse assured me. She sat me more upright to allow me to cough while she held a tissue and wiped my mouth.

"Jill," Dr. Sol's voice pulled me back to the present. She paused a moment and repeated her question, "Can you tell me what you remember?"

I opened my eyes again and stared at the ceiling. What do I remember? Remember about what? I felt my forehead wrinkle in thought as my brain tried to dig up a memory. All that I had been told so far was that I was in the Rockland County Medical Center and that I had been in an accident.

"How long have I been here?" I countered.

"It will be a week tomorrow," she replied. "Today is October 28, 1995."

October, I thought, fall. Leaves, I remember leaves. Rain and leaves. Slippery leaves on the road. I was driving home, tired. "Leaves, and rain," I shared with her. I strained my thought processes more. Tired, I remember feeling very tired. Work. It hit me, work. I had just finished a long double shift. Karen, one my unit's veteran nurses, was telling me to avoid Route 9 there because there was a big accident, take the back roads home. Uggh, I remember thinking, all I want to do is get home and get into my bed.

"Where are you with the leaves and rain?" Dr. Sol again, redirecting my thoughts.

"In my car, driving, driving home from the hospital

on Old Kelly Road." No coma could make anyone forget Old Kelly Road. It was lined with big old oak trees right along its edges, only the locals used it. "It was windy."

"Good, very good," Dr. Sol leaned back in her chair just a little and pushed that strand of hair behind her ear. "What else do you remember?"

It took several minutes for me to recount what I could remember: working a double shift even though my gut told me not to, the night nurses warning me about the accident on Route 9 and the slippery roads; feeling tired and wanting to get home.

"Anything else, anything else while you were driving?" she hinted.

I looked into her eyes and saw there was more, but for the life of me, I couldn't find in my head what it was.

"No," feeling like a game contestant who couldn't answer the million dollar question. "The next thing I remember is being here."

Dr. Sol glanced over at my parents concerned.

"What, what aren't you telling me?" I pulled myself more upright, my right side wasn't happy.

"Jill, you were in a car accident." Dr. Sol stated.

I looked at her trying to find a memory of this. "Did I hit one of those big oak trees?" that would make the most sense.

Dr. Sol braced herself a bit, swallowed, and responded, "No, Jill, you hit another car. The car had passengers in it."

Passengers. Immediately my stomach tightened and so did my hands. "Are they OK?"

Then the bomb, which Dr. Sol dropped as gently as she could, but it was way too heavy for any one person to carry. "The other car had a young couple in it. The wife was pregnant, they were on their way to the hospital to deliver their baby." She paused for a brief second to let my mind absorb this, then, rather than prolong the agony, continued. "Jill, the parents were killed in the collision. The baby was delivered emergently and lived."

The pain in my right side was immediately trumped by the punch to my stomach. Killed, I killed a newborn baby's parents! I go to work everyday trying to comfort or help people get better, live, yet, in an instant, I killed two people and left a newborn baby an orphan?

Chapter 6

HELEN

OCTOBER 28, 1995

"I don't understand why that damn hospital had Jill working for 16 hours! Don't these nurses work hard enough just on one shift!" My husband, William, bypasses the rotating exit doors and slams open the handicap-only door. My son, Billy, and I follow behind.

I know there is no point in trying to say anything when William is in this kind of ranting mood. Which is a relief, actually, because I don't know where to start.

We all got into the car, William starts it and just sit quietly, and stare straight ahead. The black shiny Acura hums quietly. The vanilla air freshener that he keeps stuffed under the passenger seat is making me feel nauseous. I use every ounce of willpower I have not to reach down, grab it and throw it out the window. The thought of adding any more stress to the situation prevents me from doing so.

William tunes out, rather than putting the car into gear and driving us home. I sneak a peak at Billy sitting in the back seat. His eyes meet mine, only for a second, and say without words, "I don't know."

Finally, William breaks his stare; his head falls into the steering wheel and stays there. He begins sobbing, uncontrollably, while repeating, "My poor baby girl, my poor baby girl." In all our years of marriage, 28 years next June, I have only seen him like this one other time. Tears come to my eyes too, but I held onto them tight. Someone needs to stay strong.

I gently reach over and stroke his back, "She'll be OK, she is a very strong girl!"

As I say this, a pair of young kids dressed in Halloween costumes follows their mother through the parking lot like ducklings. One dressed as a witch, the other a big fat orange pumpkin. I admire the creativity that went into the costumes, each obviously custom made.

I used to make all of the kids' costumes when they were young. Jill always wanted to be some version of a princess that was, until, the "tragedy" happened. One year, we picked out pink velvet material and I sewed her the perfect pink princess dress. I added three layers of tulle under it to make the skirt extra puffy. She insisted we make a crown, which started as a challenge, but I figured out a way to make one out of her headband. She and I glued at least a hundred rhinestones to the tiara to make it really glitter. When all was said and done, her costume was more ornate than a Christmas ornament and her dress more elegant than most wedding gowns. Those were the days, I think to myself.

After the tragedy, we were in a local department store getting Jill some sneakers to go to school with. There was a rack of costumes by the cashier. Jill perused the rack while I waited in line.

"What kind of costume is this?" she pulled the white dress with white hat and make believe medical bag all attached off the rack and held it. She peered into the medical bag.

"That's a nurse costume," I told her.

"What's a nurse?" she put the costume back on the rack, but kept looking at it.

"Someone who helps people who aren't well get all better," I said.

"I want to be a nurse this Halloween," she said firmly.

"OK, we can make you a nurse costume," I said as I placed the sneakers on the cashiers counter.

The cashier smiled at Jill, "Nurses are very special people!"

Jill beamed, showing her newly missing front tooth. "Well, that's what I am going to be for Halloween!"

From that day on Jill wanted to be a nurse not just on Halloween, but when she grew up.

William lifts his head off the wheel, tilts it back and takes a deep, heavy breath. "At least she's alive," he says as he looks over at me, his face wet with tears. Thank God for that. I reach into the glove compartment and fish through the stack of maps and oil change receipts in hope of finding a packet of tissues. William wipes the tears with the sleeve of his burgundy cashmere sweater. The same one he wore yesterday. The scruff on his face snags along the luxurious wool. The last time I saw him with any resemblance of a beard was several years ago, when he returned from a guys fishing trip.

"What do you think, I think I will try growing a beard!" he said triumphantly.

I scrunched my nose up in disgust. The look on his face sunk. "No beard, huh?"

"No beard," I replied. "I like my man clean shaven and as smooth as a baby's bottom."

"While you two were with Jill and that shrink, I heard the nurse talking to one of the doctors about possibly transferring Jill out of the ICU to a regular floor soon." Billy pipes in.

"Thank God she's alive," William repeats and starts the car.

"Thank God is right," I say. God must have heard me that night. Soon after I awoke from the nightmare the phone rang at 12:32 am.

"Helen?" A man's deep voice asked.

"Yes, who is this?" I replied.

"It's Ray," our friend on the police department replied.

"Ray, is something wrong?" I sat straight up in the bed again, alone, and reached over to turn the light on. I figured William must have fallen asleep on the couch again watching his late night comedy shows.

"Helen, we normally wait until we know more to call, but I know you would want to know right away." He paused only briefly. "I am at the scene, the paramedics are working to get your daughter out of the car. There has been an accident."

"An accident!" I screamed. "Is she all right?"

"She's breathing, I know that, they are going to take her to Rockland Medical Center. It would be best if you meet us there."

I slammed the phone down, from what I can remember and jumped out of bed. "NO!!!! NO!!!!! God, you cannot have my daughter!"

William bolted in my room, still dressed in his clothes from the day before. "What's going on?"

"It's Jill. She's been in an accident. They are taking her to Rockland Medical Center."

If we had any discussion on the ride to the hospital, I don't remember what it entailed. Our thoughts were so determined to find our daughter OK; there was no time to divert them.

When we entered the ER, Ray spotted us from across the room. He immediately came to us and ushered us to the left. "Jill is over here. Please wait here and do not leave this area without letting me know." Ray looked at us concerned, then looked behind him to an area on the other side of the emergency room. A young woman with long jet black hair maybe in her twenties stood, holding onto two adults, both with gray hair near two closed curtains. Emergency staff scattered around like mice, gathering supplies, screaming orders, and wheeling medical devices to the two sides of the ER. I didn't think anything of Ray's instructions, more like orders, at the time. I was just glad that I was close to my daughter. I wonder if that group of people on the other side of the ER knew who we were.

Chapter 7

JILL

NOVEMBER 1, 1995

I looked over at the windowsill filled with flower arrangements. The big basket in the center overflowed with crisp, fall colored mums. They looked like they were starting to wilt. Note to self: ask the next visitor who arrives to add water to that flower arrangement. I knew the next visitor would not be my dad. He and my brother were at my apartment packing up my things. My landlord agreed to let me out of my lease given the situation with just a one-month penalty. Since the apartment was on the second floor, only accessible by stairs, it was unrealistic to expect that I could get back there and live alone any time soon.

The knee length cast on my right leg was covered with get-well wishes. The doctors were optimistic that the two fractures, one in my tibia and the other in my fibula, would heal and I would make a full recovery, but it would take time. I had figured out what angles and how many pillows it took to position my leg so it didn't hurt. My right clavicle was another story. The hairline fracture it sustained was not severe enough to operate on. My doctors ordered me to try to limit the mobility as much as possible so that it would just heal on its own. In order to do this, I had to keep my right arm in a sling. Needless to say, with two appendages out, and being right side dominant, my ability to function and take care of things on my own was encumbered.

Being so dependent on other people was not my style. I was the one who was supposed to be helping other people. The feeling of powerlessness was compounded by the sadness I felt for the newborn baby with no parents. As much as I tried, I could not remember the moment of impact or even seeing another car on the road as people were telling me there was. The police were still investigating and had not yet issued a report on who or what was to blame for the accident. To me, it didn't matter what the report would say. I already blamed myself. If I had not been there that night, if I had not stayed to work that double shift as my inner voice had tried to warn me, if I….The list of reasons why it was my fault grew longer the more I sat trapped in the hospital. I wanted to go to the maternity ward and see the baby, to tell her how sorry I was. I was strictly forbidden. The baby's extended family specifically requested that I not be allowed. I was told that she went home with her mother's sister who would be adopting her.

I wanted to get out of the hospital too. The plan for me, however, was to go to the rehab floor first and then my parents' home as we discussed in a recent family meeting. I was beginning to feel like my life was going backward.

My flowers had a chance at survival because Becky came to visit at lunchtime. After watering my plants, she set my lunch tray up in front of me. She was such a welcome sight. I wished I were in Riverview Hospital where more of my friends from my unit could have visited. Riverview, however, was just a community hospital. They didn't have the specialized care I needed.

With my left hand, I fed myself. Becky sat on the chair near the window and took out her turkey sandwich from a brown paper lunch bag and a bottle of water.

"When do you go to rehab?" Becky asked. She got up to pull the window curtain closed a bit because she noticed me squinting from the bright sun shining its rays right into my eyes.

"Thanks for blocking that," I said. "They're talking about in the next two or three days. They're just waiting for a bed to open up."

"That's great! You will be another step to getting better!" Becky tilted her head as she realized what she said, "No pun intended."

I smiled.

"Hey, remember that guy that I was telling you about who contacted me on the dating website?"

I nodded my head as my fork full of hot open-faced turkey sandwich half made it into my mouth, the other half plopped on the towel covering my chest.

"Well, after emailing back and forth, we spoke on the phone last night. He sounds really nice! He lives with a roommate in Hoboken. He's a computer programmer. We are going to meet at The Wine Bar in Piermont on Saturday." Becky blushed.

"That's great!" I tried to sound equally as excited. I was thrilled for Becky, I really was. At the same time, sitting around all day made me think of Jack more than I wanted to. Adding to my physical and emotional injuries of this whole episode was my beaten up ego, also black and blue. Jack didn't come to visit, didn't phone, and didn't even send a get well card.

I pushed Jack out of my thoughts, "So, what are you going to wear?"

"I was thinking about the grass green dress, you

know, the one that matches my eyes?"

"That's a good choice, you look good in that," I said as I picked up the milk carton, the kind they serve you in grammar school, and ripped it open with my teeth.

"You could have asked me to open that for you," Becky chided.

"I know, thanks, but the more I do for myself, the sooner I'll get better."

"So, what else do you know about this guy? What's his name again, Jim?"

"Well, he grew up in Virginia, near Richmond. He went to school at NYU then decided the money was better up here so he stayed. He works at a firm in Manhattan." Becky took a break and sipped from her water bottle. "Would you believe he says that someday soon we'll be doing all of our patient documenting on a computer?"

"No, but I hope that the computers can document the patient's condition on their own so we don't have to waste so much time charting about patients; we can actually take care of them!" I retorted.

"Yea, that would be great! I will have to ask Jim about that." Becky continued on sharing what she had gathered about Jim just from phone and email. Jim enjoyed the outdoors, although he was not dedicated to one sport. He was the oldest of three brothers, which Becky liked because she was the youngest in her family so she felt they wouldn't clash with control issues. Besides, she kind of liked the idea of her guy being more the leader, the caretaker. She wanted kids someday, and she felt she wanted the freedom to focus on being a mother, without having to worry about being a breadwinner too.

"Well, he sounds like a good guy so far. Have you seen any other pictures than his profile picture?" I asked.

"No, and to be honest, I'm kind of worried about that." Becky confided. "His profile picture was taken from a distance. He looks like he has short, shaggy, dirty blond hair, but I can't see the detail of his face too well. The picture only shows him from the chest up in which he looks well built, muscular. I hope to God that he doesn't have a huge beer belly!"

I laughed as I waved a fork at her. "Just remember, this is only a date. If it's bad or he isn't quite what you had in mind, you don't have to go out again. If it is really bad, excuse yourself to go to the bathroom and run away!"

Becky held her hand to her full mouth and tried to swallow. "Oh, I couldn't do that, that would be mean."

I worried sometimes about Becky, her sweet, southern style, living here, near the city of vultures.

Sensing my concern, Becky waved her hand back at me, "Now don't you go worrying. I have already briefed my roommates on where I am going, showed them Jim's profile and what time I expect to be home. Julia doesn't have any plans that night so she said she would wait up until I get home."

"I'm sure everything will be just fine," I didn't want to leave Becky's exciting evening on a negative note. "I want to hear all about it on Saturday!"

Becky tossed her lunch waste in the trashcan and collected the remaining debris from around my tray and put the tray on the rack in the hall. I rolled up the towel that I had made into a bib and placed on my chest before lunch. Just a small chunk of the hot turkey, a little bit of milk, and a blob of red Jell-O were on it. I was getting better at eating with my left hand.

"I'm sorry I have to run, my car needs to be inspected." Becky slung her purse over her shoulder, and then stood at my bedside. "I have to work 12 hour shifts the next two days, then a dayshift on Friday, so I won't be able to get back to see you until the weekend."

"Hopefully, I will get up to the rehab floor by then. They tell me I will be working pretty intensely, so that will keep me busy. Tell everyone at work that I say Hi," I forced a grin. "Have a great time on your date, I can't wait to hear about it!"

Becky deserved only my best wishes even though I wasn't really in the mood to feel cheery. Becky gave me a gentle hug and left. Her fresh scent lingered. I would need to ask her what type of perfume that is; it smelled nice.

"You don't find guys like Jack all the time," my mother's voice reminded me again. I thought about my mother. It was rather odd that my mom said she had a lot of errands to do that day, so she wouldn't be in to visit. The day before she said she had a lot of laundry to do. I imagined that things did indeed get backed up at home since my accident interrupted all of our lives. But it was just she and my dad—how much laundry could two people generate? And didn't she worry and want to come and see me?

I heard someone knock on my door, another unscheduled interruption. I needed to get better fast I thought to myself. These constant interruptions at all hours of the day and nights were wearing on me. How do patients actually get better in a hospital? I was really beginning to wonder.

"May I come in?" It was Dr. Sol. She wore a tweed jacket with a crisp white collared shirt underneath and dark blue wool skirt with low heeled rider-like boots. Her tight curled shoulder length hair was loose today, not pulled back the way she normally wore it. She looked younger that way.

"Sure, come on in," I invited her. She would help kill another half hour or so.

Soap operas were never my thing, nor was the *Price is Right.* I didn't have the concentration lately to read any of the books piled up on my bedside table, and I only had one magazine left I hadn't leafed through.

"Thank you," she entered, pulled a chair up to the side of my bed and sat down.

"Your hair looks good like that, I haven't seen you wear it down, " I commented.

"Thank you," she gently smiled. That was as much as I would get from her. Being a psychiatrist, her job was to let me talk, not the other way around.

"So, how are you feeling today?" she asked.

"Restless, maybe that's a good sign. I'm getting antsy, I want to get up and do things, I want to get out of here."

"That is good to hear. You will need that kind of energy to start working on your rehab." She looked down and smoothed a wrinkle out of her skirt. I knew this meant we were going to talk about something potentially uncomfortable. As much as Dr. Sol tried to be a pillar of strength, the accident and the implications it left, were hard for any human being to think about. Any human being, at least, who had a heart.

She looked me in the eye again. "The police completed their investigation." She didn't dance around a subject; she came straight to the point. I liked that about her. My parents agreed that she would be the lead point person to keep me abreast of the news involving the other family and the accident. This would allow my parents to be able to focus on being parents and for me to get this difficult information from one source.

I held my breath. As I said, it didn't matter what the

police found, I killed those two people in my mind. The question was, would everyone else agree?

"A witness came forward after he saw the news of the accident on TV. Apparently, he was on the same road that you all were that night, just a quarter mile or so ahead of you. He said that he almost hit the couple's car as well, they swerved into his lane." She continued. "Since you have no recollection of the accident, the police are unclear if you fell asleep at the wheel or have just wiped out your memory of the impact. From what they have gathered, they believe the wife was laying down in the backseat of the car. The husband must have been distracted by the contractions. The ER report showed she was very dilated and the baby was already crowning."

I released my breath as Dr. Sol finished. "Since the impact was right in the center of the road, they aren't quite sure what happened, but there is evidence that it could have been either of you straying from your lane or both. Since there is no evidence of recklessness, they are concluding it as a No-Fault accident."

No Fault, it wasn't no fault, it was my fault! Dr. Sol even said they passed by another driver and didn't collide.

"There will be no criminal charges. I do have to warn you, however, that the family of the baby have threatened to file a civil suit." She paused and gave me a chance to react.

"So that means they would sue me for money?" I asked. "I will give it to them, all that I have for that baby."

"Jill, you cannot carry the blame for this." Dr. Sol straightened up, stronger now. "This was an accident, an unfortunate act of timing. These things happen in life, and very often we have no way of explaining why."

I stayed silent, letting her think she was getting her

point across to me.

"There is something else that you should know." she softened again. "I got a call from one of Riverview Hospital's attorneys. Some of the Hospital's Board of Directors want to know what your state of mind was, whether you used good professional judgment staying on for that extra shift."

Now I was livid. My blood boiled. "You've got to be kidding! I can handle bearing the responsibility for the sake of that baby and her family, but this wouldn't have happened if the hospital staffed themselves properly!"

"Apparently, the hospital is getting a lot of negative press on this situation. It is not unusual for big firms like this to try to spin it and find a scapegoat." She sighed. "Again, I need you to know this is not your fault. I just thought you should be aware of this other information."

My right clavicle area began to burn. Clenching my muscles probably put pressure on the fractured area. I wanted to get out of my bed and go for a power walk. Just walk and let my mind shuffle all the thoughts that were rotating in my head. Sitting there, stuck in that bed, was just letting them rotate like colliding funnel clouds.

"How do you feel about all this?" an open ended question, meant for me to take the conversation in any direction that I wanted. We had learned about this technique in Psych 101.

I looked away, out the window. "I don't know." I said. But I did know. I felt betrayed.

Chapter 8

HELEN
NOVEMBER 1, 1995

There must be another cord that connects a mother to her children, I think to myself. An invisible cord, that cannot be cut, like the umbilical one.

There are times when I am grateful for this. The instinctive knowing that has allowed me to deter my kids from harm, catch them in the act of fibbing, or bask in their feelings of joy that come when they overcame challenges. I admit, however, today I wish I had a magic pair of scissors to cut this cord.

The nausea poking at me coupled with relentless fatigue is colliding with my worry about Jill. I know she is longing for me to visit her. I must tell her the truth, before she ends up dead. This whole tragic accident probably never would have happened if it were not for me, and my stupidity.

I begin to try to summon up the courage to figure out how to set Jill free, but nausea takes over and I have no choice but to give in to it.

Exhausted and woozy, I return to the couch in the den. Maybe if I watch TV it will distract me. I long to just lie down and take a nap. Lord, please give me the strength I am going to need to help Jill when she comes back home.

I wrap the blue and white afghan that I knit around me and put my head down on the square pillow that matches the couch. Oh, how I miss my old knitting club! Those were the days. My friends and I would send our kids off to school and then gather at one anothers' homes for tea and a treat while we knit. We nicknamed ourselves the "Stitch and Bitch Club." We never really meant anything by our bitching. It was a safe haven for us to vent our frustrations and share our fears. Kids who didn't clean up after themselves, husbands who didn't call when they would be late for dinner, worried about elderly parents whether they could safely drive anymore.

We shared recipes, proud achievements our kids had, and fashion tips too. All the while we stitched away. I was more of a knitter. Clara, an expert in the craft, coached me beyond my knit one, pearl two, Afghans. Over the years I came to knit my own sweaters, the kids' hats and mittens, and even warm wool socks. There were other knitters in our group who preferred crochet or needlepoint. I still have a beautiful crocheted doily on the side table here next to me from Martha. God bless, Martha. I hope she is doing OK. Last I heard she was living in a nursing home near her kids who lived in Massachusetts after being diagnosed with MS.

As much as we tried to keep the group together, it was hard as the kids got older. Our daily routines changed. Some of us went back to work. Some moved away. Some got sick. One of us, Dawn, already passed away.

Dawn was always the joker in the group. She kept us laughing with her silly antics. Even when she got breast cancer her sense of humor never waned. "Laughter is the best medicine!" she professed. She wore all kinds of silly wigs when she lost her hair. Pink punk hair, dreadlocks, flowing long blond, curly brunette, she had one for every mood and occasion. She was so full of life none of us believed she could possibly die. When she did, we were devastated. We felt forced to look at our own mortality.

Our stitching club knit baby hats and blankets for the local hospital in her honor. Dawn would have liked that. I still smile every time I look at her doily. She's on my list of people that one day I hope to see again.

REHAB

Chapter 9

JILL

NOVEMBER 14, 1995 MORNING

"You are doing really well, Jill," Josh, my physical therapist, watched me anchor my specially adapted walker and then sit in the blue pleather hospital chair.

I had to admit, I wouldn't have predicted that in just two weeks I would be able to sponge bathe, dress myself and hobble to the bathroom. I had to channel all the uncontrollable elements going on in my life into something. It may as well have been getting better.

"Thanks, Josh, couldn't do it without you." I cheered him on as much as he cheered for me. "They are talking about sending me home next week. My family is fixing up the den downstairs so I won't have to maneuver the stairs with this cast."

"Great, I want to work on some strength training exercises with you tomorrow that you can then do on your own. It'll help you walk faster once the cast is off. It's important not to just let your muscles waste away." Josh picked up his clipboard and headed for the door.

"I'll be ready," I smiled, "Bring it on!"

Left alone in my rehab room my smile faded. I sighed deeply. Sure, I had the chutzpa to get better, probably faster than the average person because I knew what it would take to heal and where to focus my energy. But, for what, I found myself asking. I didn't want to be a burden on my family, that much I knew. But, what was there to motivate me, pull me forward? What did I have to look forward to? I had no boyfriend,

no apartment of my own anymore, and a career I wasn't sure I wanted.

Why did I want to be a nurse anyway? That Talking Heads song played in my head, "Once in a Lifetime" or "How did I get here?"

Before the tornado of thoughts swirling in my head took over, I forced them into the basement shelter. My nurse manager, Marie, was scheduled to come at lunchtime today to visit. Maybe that would help, give me something to focus on for the future.

"I made you your favorite pumpkin bread," my mom entered my room carrying a foil wrapped brick. She was a welcome sight, especially carrying her infamous pumpkin bread. I smelled it as soon as she walked in.

"Wow, thanks, Mom!" Just the thought of it warmed my stomach. I pulled my table tray over across my lap. "Do you mind if I have a piece now?"

"No, not at all, I made it for you to eat, not look at," she handed it over to me and then pulled a chair over close to mine. She took her plaid wool coat off and hung it on the back of the chair. She looked thinner. A twang of guilt hit me; all the stress of my accident must really be affecting her.

I unwrapped the end of the loaf. It was still warm. Under my tray table was a small drawer, I slid it open and pulled out an extra set of silverware I had stashed in there. "Would you like a piece?" I asked my mother without looking up.

"Oh no, that is for you, honey," she replied. "I baked

a batch of them. I stored some in the freezer for when you get home. I made a couple for Dad to take to the office, too."

As I sank my teeth into the warm, moist bread I was transported home. Home, meaning the place where I grew up, and the place I was going back to. The comfort of that began to sink in. Perhaps nestling back into the nest is just what I needed. At least for now until I could figure out what I needed to do next with my life. What a mess.

"You know, most of those ladies don't have time to cook for themselves," my mother was still talking about the agents in Dad's office.

My father owned the most successful real estate brokerage in town. He never went to college. He worked as an assistant in the real estate firm Buxnell & Turner in high school, doing odds and ends in the office. The owners took a liking to my dad, as most people did. He was highly personable and good-looking, or so some women have told me.

"They all work so hard for Dad," my mother continued.

My father got his real estate license as soon as he got out of high school. With his knowledge of our town, extroverted personality and charm, he was off to the races. Being first to know what valuable properties came on the market worked in his favor as well. The locals who decided to sell their properties always came to him first, and if he was willing to buy it himself, they didn't mind selling it to him. He was known to give them a better than appraisal payout and save them the aggravation of putting it on the market. It was a win-win, my father always said.

When it came time to sell the firm the partners, Buxnell and Turner, offered it to dad first. They had acquired more than enough to retire and were willing to sell it to my father at a fair price. My parents had recently married and my mom was pregnant with me. It was a stretch for them, financially, but they felt it was worth the sacrifice and a deal was made. The sacrifice turned out to be more than financial. Owning the business now required even more time and focus to keep the business productive. Dinners out with clients, Rotary Club meetings, charity events, every contact made with someone was a potential business transaction.

Mom didn't work, well, she did, as a wife and then a mother, and she worked very hard at that. She catered to our every need, kept beautiful gardens including ones that yielded produce like the pumpkin used for the pumpkin bread that I was now slicing a second piece of. As I did, I noticed the center of the remaining part of the loaf was raw. This was so unlike Mom. She had baked this recipe every fall as long as my memory held.

I looked up at my mother, still chatting away about the ladies in Dad's office. Again, I noticed something looked different. As I studied her, it hit me, her coloring. Something was off with her skin color.

When she paused for a breath, I asked, very matter of fact, "Hey, Mom, are you wearing a new type of makeup?" Followed by, "This bread is delicious! It really hits the spot! I am going to wrap up the rest and save it for later." I didn't have the heart to tell her it wasn't thoroughly cooked.

I caught her off guard and she touched her cheek. "Um, yes. Aunt Terri and I went over to Bloomingdales for lunch last week. They were offering free makeovers at one of the cosmetic counters. I really liked how the woman made up my face so I bought this foundation. Do you like it?"

"It looks nice," I replied, trying to hide my suspicion. I knew my mother better. She might go to a ladies lunch when everything in our lives was going well, but she certainly wouldn't go when one of her family was in the hospital. Foundation, what was she trying to cover up?

"Well, I'm glad you like the bread." She stood up. I didn't want her to go. "I'm going to run back home now and see how your father and brother are arranging things. We cleaned out the den last night; they were supposed to bring your bed down this morning. The hospital is going to provide us with a commode in case you can't make it into the hallway bathroom."

"I appreciate your help, Mom, from all of you," I really did. As bad as things were, I was very blessed to have my family's support right now. The last thing I wanted to be is one of those patients that we joke has a mailbox outside their hospital room.

She reached over and kissed me on the cheek and I kissed her back. Her scent even smelled different. She still wore her favorite perfume, Joy, but underneath it was something odorous, almost rotten smelling. The kind of smell that you get just a whiff of when you open the fridge door after you've left something in there a little too long.

"I think your brother is coming to see you tonight." She picked up her jacket and draped it over the arm carrying her matching purse. "I will try and come back tomorrow."

"OK," I said. "Thank you again for the bread." Try? What was she so busy doing all of a sudden that she couldn't conclusively say she would be back tomorrow?

Chapter 10

HELEN

NOVEMBER 14, 1995

"Leaving so soon?" the secretary sitting at the nurses' station asks me as I head towards the exit door.

"Yes, I need to go home and get the house ready for my daughter's return." I toss back with a smile, without stopping.

I make it through the door to the elevator bay just in time. Thankfully no one else is there. I bend over and beg God not to let me throw up or pass out. I give it a few seconds and my prayers are answered. Thank you, God.

I reach over and hit the down arrow. It's on its way up, only two floors to wait, I can do this. It kills me not to be with my daughter right now. I know she is starting to suspect something; she's always been a smart one. My son, Billy, on the other hand, doesn't seem to notice anything different. I guess that is why they call it women's intuition.

I'm not ready to tell Jill yet. No need to burden her with my troubles. I need her to focus on getting better. But, I don't know how much longer I will be able to keep this from her.

The elevator opens, an elderly woman and a doctor get out. Neither holds the door open, but I get in on time and hit the button for the first floor. I don't make it down to the ground level alone, the elevator nearly fills as it stops like the local train to Grand Central picking a few up here and there.

The hospital lobby is bustling. Visitors arriving, patients being wheeled out to the pick up area, doctors and staff gathered in the food courtyard having late morning coffee. I stop in the hospital gift store, maybe a hard candy will help ease my stomach.

The gift store is filled with beautiful flower arrangements neatly made, ready to go, magazines and books, and a dedicated section just for newborns. The pink and blue teddy bears line up on a table next to the rack of soft cotton onesies, baby blankets and hats. I still have the knit hats and blankets my mother-in-law made for Jill and Billy to leave the hospital with when they were born. Jill's was pure white with silk ribbon woven in along the edges. Billy's was yellow and white since his due date was in the spring. Back then we didn't have a choice to find out what the sex of the baby would be so gifts in pink or blue didn't usually come until after the baby was born.

I wonder if my pregnancies would have been different had I chosen to know their sexes while I carried them. I think not, that was part of the excitement! And God knows there was enough to think about preparing for the arrivals. Breast or bottle feed, what diaper service to use, preparing ready-to-eat meals to store in the freezer to ease the load after the birth. No, I am glad I didn't find out. I am actually glad that I didn't have many of the choices that women have today. Life just seemed simpler back then in the 70s.

I pick up one of the pink teddy bears and hold its soft fur to my cheek. I close my eyes for a moment and the tenderness and love that filled my heart when I first held my baby girl returned. I open my eyes and pull the bear away and we stare at each other eye to eye. The bear's eyes are tender, like it senses my woes. As foolish as it sounds, I buy the bear, along with the hard candy. I tell myself it will be a comfort gift for Jill when she returns home. In reality, however, I'm not sure if it will be she or me who needs the bear more.

Chapter 11

JILL

NOVEMBER 14, 1995 AFTERNOON

Marie entered my room at 2pm sharp, just as I knew she would. Her dark brunette hair was pulled back in a bun as always. Her deep brown eyes looked soft, but I knew they had the power to turn razor fierce at any time.

"Look at you sitting up in that chair, you're looking good!" she sounded somewhat surprised. Little did she know that I put extra effort into looking more like a normal person, rather than a patient today. I donned a little mascara, put my hair in a ponytail and wore an extra large cardigan sweater over my hospital gown, in lieu of a bathrobe.

"Thanks, come on in, grab a seat," I pointed towards the same chair my mother sat in earlier this morning. After she pulled the chair up, closer to me than my mother did, she handed me a bright yellow gift bag with pink tissue paper popping out of it. "A little gift from the staff."

"That's sweet, shall I open it now?"

"Sure, go ahead," she replied.

Deep inside the bag was a two-piece, white cotton pajama set with little roses dotted throughout. It was from Crabtree & Evelyn, Becky must have told them I love that store. Complementing it was a lovely bath set also from the same. There was a card on the bottom. "Wishing you well, from all of us!" It said on the outside and inside, "Get well fast!" surrounded by signatures and well wishes. I put the card and gifts back in the bag for now. I would read it more thoroughly later.

"Wow, that is very sweet of everyone," I said.

"They are all thinking of you." She replied and ended it there. Isn't she supposed to add, "and they can't wait for you to get back"?

"So, how are things going, how do you feel?" Marie asked.

"Good, we are making plans for me to go home soon." I shared. "How are things on the unit?"

Marie caught me up on the latest news that was publicly known. Tisha had the baby, a boy, 7 pounds, 6 ounces. Cindy announced she would be retiring at the end of the year. Lorraine got back from her honeymoon in Tahiti. The Joint Commissions report came back mostly positive for the hospital. They cited our unit mostly for missing documentation.

"I better get back soon before I really get out of the loop," I jested.

Marie looked at me concerned. Now what, I thought.

"Well, that is part of the reason that I am here, Jill." She looked briefly at the floor, then back at me. "The hospital board has asked me to prepare a report as to whether or not I think you are able to return."

After what Dr. Sol told me, this didn't come as a total surprise. What did surprise me, however, was the look on Marie's face that seemed to say, "I'm not sure what to say".

"You look like you're not sure yourself," I put the cards on the table.

"Jill, you know that I think you're an awesome nurse.

One of the best that we have in fact," she bit the underside of her lip. "But, and we have talked about this before, sometimes you are too good, go too far to help your patients."

Yes, we had spoken about this before. Like the time I offered to help a trauma patient leave the hospital to view her brother's wedding ceremony without asking my manager first. By the time my manager heard of my offer, the patient and her family were so excited Marie felt like she had no choice but to say yes. In the end, she pulled strings to get the hospital insurance to cover me while we left the hospital for a couple of hours, but it was a risk. Then there were the times, occasionally, when I would clash with other staff members because they didn't perform, in my eyes, in the patients' best interests. Like the time when Cleo, one of our senior nurses' aides, wouldn't wash a patient's hair on the evening shift. "That's for the day shift," she told me adamantly when I asked her to wash a patient's hair who had been bypassed for several days on the day shift because of higher acute needs. Maybe Cleo was right; they were better staffed to do that on days, but it wasn't getting done.

"You have very high standards for the way you take care of patients," she continued, "and most of the time it yields incredible results for them. But, not everyone is able to perform at that level. And sometimes, you go overboard."

I knew Marie was struggling with this. It was she who nominated me for Nurse of the Year during Nurse Week last year. It was she who always gave me the highest rating she could on my yearly performance review. I think she had hoped that discussing my overzealousness would tame it. And if I were honest with myself, there were times when I, too, wished I could tune it down. I couldn't explain why I had this drive deep inside me to help patients get better, to save them. I hated to see them suffer, or worse, die, even if it was at the expense of my needs. And I could be demanding on my colleagues, wanting them be part of my effort.

Normally, I would have loudly objected to what she was saying. I would have countered with something like, "Well, are you going to put in your report that if the hospital board better appreciated what we nurses do and added more staff we wouldn't have incidents like this?" This time, however, I just sat in silence. Why, why couldn't I be more balanced like my peers? This time my trying so hard to help killed two people and left a newborn baby an orphan. I wondered, should I, do I even want to, continue being a nurse?

Chapter 12

JILL

NOVEMBER 14, 1995 EVENING

"Wheel…of….. Fortune!" The television screamed.

I had thought about calling my brother and asking him to visit another time. Three hours of physical therapy, the visits from my mom and manager left me not only physically, but mentally, exhausted. I couldn't fight off the urge to shut my eyes, so I closed them, just for a minute, I told myself.

"Hey, Bionic Woman!" Billy startled me awake.

It was my brother, who came blasting in, not realizing I was sleeping. He tried to instill inspiration in me with the mantra from the Bionic Woman show we used to watch as kids, "We will rebuild her, make her stronger, faster."

After I realized who it was, I looked around the room. What time was it? Vanna White was still turning letters; I must have only dozed off for a few minutes.

"Oh, sorry, didn't know you were sleeping," my brother shrugged his shoulders in an oops fashion.

"No, no, it's OK, I was just resting my eyes," I waved him in.

Billy strolled in, took the same chair used by my earlier guests, but turned it around, straddled it, and sat down. "So how's it going? You ready to run 100 miles per hour yet?"

I chuckled, remembering us as kids fighting over who could run faster me or him, aka, the Six Million Dollar Man.

"Almost," I jested back, "They just need to put the supercharged batteries into my legs."

"We have your room all set up now in the downstairs den. I don't know about that commode thing, though. I draw the line at emptying that thing. You just better hustle yourself into the bathroom." He squelched his face.

I knew in my heart that my brother loved me enough that he would empty it if I really needed him to. "It's a just in case, don't worry," I smiled. I was tired of talking about my situation so I turned the conversation to him. "So what's going on in the world out there?"

"Nothing much, the usual. Chris and I went to O'Malley's last night. It was packed! They had a really good band. Some of your old high school buddies were there, Tina, Josie, Annie, and...Jack was there," Billy went silent, he obviously didn't mean to share that last bit. Looking like he was caught in a corner, he waited to see my reaction.

"Jack was there? Does he hang out a lot in Nyack? I would think he would go out in the city now that he lives there." I tried to stay calm as my stomach turned.

"Um, no, actually this is the first time I've seen him around since you guys, well you know, split up," Billy's shoulders hunched.

I felt bad for Billy. Jack and I dated so long that he was almost akin to a brother to him. Before now, I didn't really think about the fact that our breakup was a loss for him too. "What's he up to?" I felt the air growing thicker.

"Working, he says he's working hard, doing well. He

likes the city. He just came to Nyack to see his folks for the weekend." I could see Billy was leaving something out, he kept looking away from me.

"Did you tell him about what happened to me? To be honest, I'm surprised he doesn't know, he didn't even send a get well card." Luckily, the anger I felt dammed up the tears that wanted to break free.

"Umm," Billy searched for words, "Jack did hear about the accident. He thought it would better for you if he just left you alone." Billy looked torn.

"Why would he think that?" I said accusingly. Billy remained silent. Then it hit me. My stomach twisted tighter. A tear trickled down my face. "He's seeing someone else already, isn't he?

Billy put his face in his hands and slowly wiped them down to his chin. "Yeah, he is, I'm sorry, I didn't mean to bring Jack up."

I looked away, towards the window, and tried to pretend I had an itch, rather than wiping the tear away. I took a deep breath, a sip of water from the pink plastic cup that matched my water jug. I knew better than to torture myself with details, but my curiosity got the better of me. "Is she pretty?"

Billy sat silent, obviously he didn't want to go down this road, which meant that yes, she was. "Well, she's all right" he fudged.

"What does she look like?"

"You know, like a girl, blond hair, kinda tall," he shared reluctantly.

"She's pretty, isn't she? A knockout, right?" I was going to drag it out of him and he knew it. I knew at this point in Jack's life, he would be on a roll and wouldn't settle for anything else but a first place trophy girlfriend. A lucrative career only added to all the pluses he already brought to the table; he would have no trouble getting what he wanted in the Big Apple.

"If you must know, yes, she's a model, now don't ask me anymore. I really don't know anything else. The music was really loud and he left shortly after we ran into each other."

"OK, you're off the hook. "

His shoulders relaxed.

It was hard to change to a lighter subject after the Jack discussion. Billy asked me if there was anything else I needed. We watched the rest of Wheel of Fortune together. The end of the show provided the perfect segue for him to take the exit he surely wanted. He tapped me on the left leg, "Sleep tight, you'll be home in no time."

I wrenched up a smile, "Thanks, thanks for coming."

If I had the energy, I would have hobbled to the door and if it had a lock on it, I would lock it closed. Aren't visitors supposed to come to cheer patients up in the hospital? My head started swirling again. My poor brother, he came in to cheer me up and left defeated. Then my mind turned to the baby. How was her aunt dealing with the loss of a sister and an unplanned new infant to care for? I missed the camaraderie of my fellow staff members back on 7 East. They had no choice but to move on with their lives and do the work at hand. The patients never stopped coming. How long would it be before they would forget about me? Would I ever be going back, or worse, would I have the option to? And then there was my mother. I had meant to ask Billy if he noticed anything different about her.

Chapter 13

HELEN

NOVEMBER 15, 1995

For some reason I awoke feeling refreshed this morning. I sit up and let my legs dangle down the side of the bed for a moment. The old fashioned percolating coffee pot is making clanking sounds in the kitchen. It was a wedding gift we received from one of William's relatives. We have a more modern drip version, of course, but the coffee taste doesn't compare to the percolator, although it takes a lot longer to make. I stifle a chuckle at the image of William wrestling with it, trying his best to help.

The oriental carpet is radiant this morning with the bright beam of sun highlighting its jewel toned colors. For the first time, I notice the small repeated forms that outline the rim of the carpet are miniature versions of the same large image that is in the carpet's center, except in darker colors. The carpet is like a giant kaleidoscope. As the sun beam strengthens and wanes, it almost seems to move as a kaleidoscope image does.

I rise and retrieve my thick terry cloth bathrobe hanging over the armed chair that sits in the corner of my bedroom, a gift from my daughter for Christmas several years ago. "You're still wearing that!" Jill proclaimed, with her hands on her hips, one morning that she stopped by early over the summer. "I will have to get you a new one for Christmas this year."

"No, please don't," I countered. "I love it just the way it is. It's nice and warm and snuggly."

Jill just rolled her eyes.

I slide a pair of my knitted booties on each foot. These I have several of, in all different colors.

As I pull the heavy burgundy curtains back, the sun's warmth melts the stiffness from my joints. I close my eyes and soak it all in. A chirping sound interrupts my indulgent moment and I open my eyes out of curiosity to see what type of bird might be singing so beautifully at this time of year. A bright red cardinal sits perched near the batch of winterberry I have planted along my garden's edge. The cardinal is camouflaged in this picture perfect moment. I have no camera or good photography skills.

So many people forget to plant for winter interest. Had it not been for the garden club book review of Rosemary Verey's, *A Garden in Winter*, I would have been one of them. That book stimulated ideas for my garden. The extra addition of the winterberries, yellow twig dogwoods, and gold mop cypress stole the show during the gray winter months when they weren't competing with the cacophony of color that surrounded them in warmer weather. The cherry red cardinal sings his song one last time, then flies away. I will have to remember to take some cuttings of the color from the garden to help decorate our Thanksgiving table.

If I start preparing now for Thanksgiving, I may be able to pace myself to get most of it created. Although my sister, Terri, is coming with her three kids, I don't want her to have to pick up my slack. She already offered to bring all the pies and mashed potatoes. I already have pumpkin bread frozen in the freezer. I need to order a fresh turkey from the butcher in town, gather the ingredients for stuffing, and decide on what vegetables to make this year. The hardest part will be the coleslaw. It takes a lot of work to get all the vegetables shredded. If it weren't everyone's favorite part of the meal, I would consider skipping it this year. I know I would never get away for trying to pass store bought off for my own.

Jill would normally help me, but this year I know will be different. The men all go off and enter the local Turkey Trot 5K in the morning, which honestly is better than having them clogging up the kitchen picking at things. Feeling good at this moment gives me hope that I can pull this holiday off.

The surprising smell of coffee has made its way into my bedroom. I raise my eyebrows, maybe he has potential. I head down to the kitchen to applaud William on his achievement, at the same time knowing that I will need to sift the coffee to free it of the loose coffee grounds.

William is standing at the stove, mug in hand, staring at the coffee erupt in and out of the small glass bubble atop of the cover.

"Staring at it makes it percolate faster I hear," I say.

William turns and tilts his head to the side, as if to say how dare I doubt his ability. "Well, if it isn't sleeping beauty!" He puts his cup down on the counter, next to a second one waiting to be filled and comes over to gently kiss me and hold me in his arms. Its moments like these I wish would last forever.

The coffee pot percolates more ferociously until it recaptures William's attention. He turns off the flame and removes it quickly from its perch to a cooler burner. Even the handle of the pot is hot, forcing him to threaten his manliness by using a pot holder to pour the steaming brew into each cup.

I retrieve the half and half from the refrigerator and we meet at the kitchen table. "Bravo," I say as he hands me mine. I add just a drop of cream to mine and then pour enough into William's to make it light. Before taking a sip I hold it just an inch from my nose and let the aroma start to awaken me. "Smells delicious." I only get two clean sips in before I feel the coffee grinds swirling against my tongue.

"Damn it! How do you make it so that the grinds don't leak out!"

I hide behind my coffee mug, not too much to bruise his precious ego, but enough to let him know, it's not that easy being a housewife.

Over the years he would rant and rave sometimes that no one appreciated how hard he worked. The kids went to school, played with their friends, took music lessons, and went to camp. I had the life, staying at home, my schedule my own, or so he thought. These episodes usually occurred when the housing market wasn't strong and quickly went away once he was busy again. I offered a few times to get a job once the kids were in school full-time, but William always said, "No, it's best if you stay home. What if the kids need something? I make plenty for both of us."

"I'd be happy to show you tomorrow morning," I offer. "It's delicious though." And it was, even with the grinds.

William releases his scowl and basks in the approval of the flavor he created. "It's starting to slow down at the office since we are getting close to Thanksgiving. Are you sure you don't want me to stay home this morning and help you with some things?"

"Thank you, honey. Actually, I feel pretty good

today. I was planning on just finishing up the den for when Jill comes home and start preparing for Thanksgiving." William looks disappointed. "Once I get my Thanksgiving shopping list together, however, maybe you could go shopping with me to help me pick it all up."

"OK, you just let me know when you're ready. And, if there's anything you need before that, let me know."

While I greatly appreciate William's offer to help, it was generally easier to do things myself, rather than try to explain and coach someone else to do it. If I only knew how well I would be feeling day by day, hour by hour, I could get more done myself, maybe even create the whole Thanksgiving feast without any help.

Chapter 14

JILL
NOVEMBER 16, 1995

The confinement of the hospital was really starting to get to me. The staff couldn't be any nicer, but the hospital routine began making me feel like a prison inmate. My day would start with a mandatory wake up time of 6 am, complete with the clanking med cart rolling down the hall. The nurses would start shouting to Mr. Brisman, even with his new hearing aide in, not to get out of bed yet.

My day got better, however, when Rashika entered the room. "Well, good morning, Miss Jill!" Her smile as bright and jubilant as I imagined the carnival costumes are in her native Jamaica. "What are you sitting there all glum about? The sun is shining, it's time to get up and rejoice! The Lord has given us another day and a beauty at that!"

Rashika opened the bedside drawer, and pulled out the rectangular plastic wash bucket with water pitcher and cup. "I gonna set you up so you can wash yourself. Be sure you wash that sorry face off of you!" She filled the bucket with warm water at the sink, then set it before me on my bedside tray table. I gave in and readjusted my attitude.

"Now, that my girl!" She cheered. Rashika then

started to sing a hymn to herself. She placed a washcloth and two white, crunchy hospital towels beside me; another thing that irked me, no bath towels. The largest size they offered was the size of a traditional hand towel.

"I guess I'm starting to get a little wiggy in here," I offered as my excuse, but realized it was more a truth after it is said out loud.

"Oh, yes, that happens, girl! You been here a long time. How 'bout I wheel you out to the sanctuary garden after you get cleaned up? A change of scenery and some fresh air do you good!"

I dove into the wash bucket with new vigor thinking maybe today would be a better day. "That sounds wonderful! Better than anything the doctor could prescribe for me."

"OK, girl, I am going to help Tony wash up Mr. Brisman, then I be back to pick you up." Rashika resumed her hymn as she closed my door behind her.

As my hands swam in the warm bucket with the washcloth, my nurse manager, Marie's words infused into my thoughts. "You are one of my best nurses, you know that. Sometimes, though, you go too far and then you become a liability."

She was right. What in the world was wrong with me? I'm not satisfied running close to the storm. No, not me, I have to go right into the eye, let it whip me around, and spit me out. Even more pathetic, I actually think I have the ability to tame it, redirect the tornado and save the entire town that it has come to scoop up.

Where's my "off button"? Am I some kind of martyr? Or am I a narcissistic person impersonating a savior? Maybe this tragic event is some kind of pause button for me. I admitted to myself that I can no longer run. With my injury, I was now forced to think, ponder, contemplate, as much as I tried to distract my mind with magazines, crossword puzzles, and phone calls.

Exchanging the clean hospital gown for the one with a small red Jell-O stain on it added to my new sense of improvement. My hair was too ratty to leave down, the tableside mirror told me. I brushed it back with my left arm, and then slid my right arm out of its sling. Surprisingly, the fracture in my right clavicle responded only with a dull ache rather than a loud scream. Although it took longer than usual, I was able to herd my hair into the elastic band.

The handle to my door clanked and Rashika struggled to push the door open with a wheelchair. "I'm coming for you, Miss Jill! I hope you're ready!" She stopped, surveyed my transformation and nodded her approval.

"I haven't been outside since I came here," I mentioned.

"Oh, it's still the same, the sun still come up an go down while the clouds stroll on by," Rashika positioned the wheelchair and set up my walker, then allowed me to shimmy myself to a standing position. "But the air is much fresher and the crisp essence of moist autumn leaves is the fragrance of the day!"

I stood and pivoted myself into the wheelchair, proud that Rashika only had to spot me, not hold onto me with a firm grip.

I got settled in the wheelchair while Rashika bundled me with blankets. "It may be November, but it is more like early October out there today, no sense spending it all inside, we have all winter to hibernate."

As Rashika tucked the final corner behind my shoulder, I asked her the question that kept nagging at me. "How do you stay so positive and cheery?"

Rashika got behind me and began pushing me towards the door as she shared her secret. "Honey, I learned a log time ago, worry is wasted energy. What good does worrying do but to rot your insides out?" I listened intently, while I felt like a prisoner who was being led to the exit door of the jail after serving my term. "No, not me. I put my faith in the Lord! Every morning that I am blessed to open my eyes I say, 'Thank you, Lord, I can't wait to see what you have in store for me today!"

Rashika's positive attitude was infectious and I began to catch it myself. And I was not alone.

"How are you on this glorious day, Rashika?" a dark skinned pharmacist asked her with his Indian accent as he held the elevator door for us.

"Wonderful! Thanks to the Lord!" Rashika professed.

We rode down the empty elevator in comfortable silence, each of us spending time with our own thoughts. The elevator dinged and the round, white light above the door lit up with the number one in it. We exited. Rashika wound me through the first floor maze while more staff wished her a good morning.

"Rashika, are you really the mayor?" I joked with her. I could feel her lift her head with pride.

"I am going to set you right over there." Rashika told me as she rolled me over the bump in the door that separates the indoor and outdoor world. "In that box is a phone. If you need help, you just dial '0'. If I don't hear from you, I will come back in a half hour." Rashika gave some final tucks to make sure my blankets are secure around me. It was just enough to cover up the slight chill in the air.

"Sounds great to me," I confirmed.

Left alone, I was surprised to be the only one taking

advantage of this beautiful escape. Although the space was only the size of maybe 20 parking spaces, its cement-paved paths were stuffed with plant life in between. The black-eyed Susies' once vibrant mustard yellow were now fading to crusty brown. Late season mums simulated the foliage colors that probably grace the deciduous trees in the park near home. Ornamental grasses staggered in heights ranging from twice my height to just a few inches tall. Fluffy plumes swayed in the wind like dust mops and whispered softly.

The sun poked out from behind the drooping cherry tree that already performed its fabulous pink flower show this past spring. The warmth wrapped around my entire body, a welcome second blanket. Thank God it's November and not bloody hot August.

Thank God. Clearly Rashika was making an impression on me. When was the last time I stopped to think about God? Do I really believe in God? Is it something I've just gone along with because it had been fed to me since I was baptized as an infant in the Church of St. Francis? How many Sundays did I sat in that church with my family, then Jack, listening to a cloak-covered priest try and put a new twist on the same seasonal message year after year? If they didn't make us get up, get down and kneel every few minutes, we'd probably all have pressure sores on our butts.

I decided to explore the jungle I had been placed into. Again, I slid my right arm out of the sling and it still only ached. I slid each hand out of the blanket cocoon and reached down to release the brakes on each wheel. As I began to roll along the walkway, the strength of my left hand threatened to roll me off the path to the right. I slowed down and let my right arm struggle to correct the course. I only got a few feet before I needed to rest.

As I allowed the tension from my muscles to drain, I took a deep breath. I noticed the back corner of the garden was not as well kept as the front. Weeds wrestled each other for a precious stake in the limited real estate. A lone clump of Queen Anne's Lace rose above the chaos. Each of the petals held patterns around the stem like snowflakes. I picked one of the flowers and studied it. Its detailed beauty made me wonder how could there not be a God?

I rested the stem on my lap and continued on my journey. The path led me in a winding circle. I stopped again besides the flowering sedum autumn joy. Its flowers resembled heads of broccoli in a shade of mauve. A shimmer of gold in between the flowers caught my eye. Carefully, I pushed them aside and found an engraved sign that read, "Garden Sanctuary donated by Seth and Julia Rosenbaum." I could only hope they could feel how grateful I was for their contribution.

Uninvited, anger crept inside of me. Why is it that this generous gift is not better maintained? I noticed to the left of me, just a couple of blocks away a giant crane reached into the sky carrying a long beam of steel. That must be where they are building the new cancer center that they've been promoting. Thousands, maybe millions, were being spent on brick and mortar, yet they couldn't maintain this simple garden.

"Jill! Where have you gone to?" Rashika yelled from my spot of origin.

"Over here!" I yelled back from the depths of the jungle.

Rashika came around the bend. She reprimanded me for moving with a gleam in her eye that said she knew I wouldn't sit still. "I think you are ready to go home."

Chapter 15

JILL
NOVEMBER 19, 1995

I pulled the cozy, thick down comforter up closer, and tucked the edge under my chin. It was starting to get cooler, despite the radiance from the moon, but not cold enough to shut the window left open just a crack. The fresh air was a welcome retreat after spending over three weeks in a stuffy hospital. Gone were the days when you could open a window there. Suicidal and delusional patients jumping out of windows mandated that they all be secured shut.

I listened to the remaining leaves perform nature's version of wind chimes, took a long deep breath and let myself relax. Maybe this wasn't so bad, being back home with my parents. I chuckled to myself as I remembered the days, not so long ago when I couldn't wait to get out of here, be on my own, do what I wanted to do. Little did I know life would smack me around pretty good and I'd have little choice but to retreat back to the nest.

The wooden banister creaked as my father went upstairs to bed, my mother had retired over an hour ago. The antique oak floorboards outlined his journey, first to my parents' bedroom, then to the bathroom, then oddly, for the third night in a row, down the hallway to his office. Why was he working so late, I wondered. I assumed that he went to bed eventually, but I was in too deep a sleep to know it.

The grandfather clock that guarded the foyer bonged 11 times. Even though antique style was not my kind of decor, I began to realize how much I missed it. There was something comforting about being surrounded by a structure that has been on this earth longer than I.

The den, now my bedroom, was dimly lit, just enough to see the family portrait of the four of us on the far wall in front of me. It was taken in a sandy dune at Cape Cod. I think I was just 12 years old in that photo; my brother would have been around 10. Our entire family loved the beach. Most of our vacations were spent by the ocean. "Going to the sea is like pushing the 'reset' button," my mom would always say.

I wondered if my parents were lonely now that we were grown and on our own, or supposed to be. I never came back after college, I moved straight into the apartment with Jack. My brother was a natural tradesman. As soon as he finished his plumbing apprenticeship, he bought a run down house in Piermont that he planned to renovate and flip. The house was really old, but it was located high on the hill overlooking the Hudson. By the time he got done with it, he would surely make a tidy profit. My dad said he already had clients asking when it would be finished.

My bladder began to twinge and I cursed myself for having so much to drink before bedtime. The virgin commode sat just a pivot distance away from my bed. "No one wants to empty that!" my brother's voice reminded me. I weighed my choices as I swung my legs over the edge of my bed and let them dangle. Normally, I called for someone to assist me. Lately, however, I had improved and they had just been watching me. My clavicle was tolerating more weight; I was almost down to just one bum limb. I only had about one more week before my cast would come off. The doctor expected I could start trying to walk on it if the X-ray showed the bones were healed.

I pulled my silver-gray walker closer and placed it directly in front of me. I slipped my sheepskin lined moccasin slipper on my left foot. Using the positioning and push-pull maneuvers my physical therapists taught me, I hoisted myself up, stabilized myself on one leg while I gently raised my right, casted leg, an inch off the floor, and shimmied my nightgown down over my backside. Once there, I realized I should have turned the light on that sat at my bedside table. The nightlight plugged into the wall socket wasn't throwing off quite enough glow even with the full moon shining through the window opening. I'll just turn the light on that is sitting by the doorway; it's just a few steps away, I told myself, after ruling out the commode.

Lifting the walker to take the first step required more finesse when trying to do it quietly. By the third round of coordinating the swing of my left leg with my right, I felt like I had a secure rhythm. As I neared the doorway, I was a good 30 inches farther away from the table lamp than I wanted to be. I leaned on my walker and reached out my left hand. Just another inch and I could reach the dangling metal chain, pull it and see my path to the bathroom down the hall.

I lifted myself up on my toes like a ballerina to give me the tiny extra reach that I needed. As I did, I pressed the extra weight on the walker with my hip. Just as the chain was in my grasp, the walker toppled. Instinctively I grabbed the lamp, and it crashed to the floor along with me. The long glass neck of the lamp shattered. I managed to soften the blow to my shoulder and head with my arm but the walker jabbed into my left hip as I smacked onto the wall-to-wall carpet.

"Ouch!" I said in a loud whisper.

Lights from upstairs flew on and I heard quick footsteps. My father reached me first, then my mother wearing a worn flannel nightgown.

"What on earth are you doing?" my father gasped. "Are you OK?"

I rolled onto my back as I rubbed my left hip. "I think so."

"Why are you up? You know you are supposed to call one of us," my mother looked in horror at the broken lamp, then me, but didn't say anything.

"I had to go to the bathroom, I thought I could make it on my own. I didn't want to wake you." I pulled myself up to a sitting position as my father placed my walker back to a standing position.

"As long as you are not hurt, let's get you back up." My dad extended his arm and wrapped it around my left arm. "Helen, you get on the other side. On the count of three we'll stand her back up."

As they chanted, "One, two, three," I pushed up with my left leg and reached for the walker again. I got my balance then found myself face to face with my mother who no longer had her face masked with foundation. Her skin was mustard. Not a faint twinge of yellow, but Grey Poupon. Her eyes opened wider when she saw me notice this.

"Mom, why is your skin jaundiced?"

She looked away from me and towards my dad. My dad gently shrugged his shoulders in reply to my mother's pleading eyes. Defeated, she turned back to me. "I have cancer."

***

I sat down on the hand woven chair, while my mother filled the green kettle. The blue and white china clock that resembled a plate ticked away above our heads. Once my father had finished helping me to the kitchen, after I finally got to the bathroom, my mother had shooed him back to bed, telling him, "You have to get up early for work, I will talk with Jill." My father didn't object. He carted the heavy bags under his eyes up the stairs.

"I haven't known for long, just a couple of weeks, " my mom poured the steaming water into a flowered tea pot, the matching tea cups sat ready at my place set and hers. "Dr. Siegel has scheduled several tests and he is looking into what the best option will be for me. I have another appointment with him on Tuesday." She said this, remarkably, very matter of fact.

Ignorance really must be bliss, I thought to myself. I did my best to follow Mom's lead so as not to panic her. Pancreatic cancer, no, not that one! How many patients did I watch go through what seemed like torture—surgery, radiation, chemotherapy, special stents, tubes, only to loose the battle and usually quickly. I felt like someone whacked me in the chest when my mother told me. I was too stunned to cry.

"I want to go with you," I insisted.

"OK, the appointment is at 10 o'clock," she dumped a lump of sugar in her tea and passed the sugar bowl over to me.

I wanted to scream. How can you be so calm? Don't you know you are going to die! But, I stifled myself. No, I would not think like that, despite knowing the odds. No, there has to be some kind of treatment for her, maybe something I didn't know about.

My hand quivered as I transferred the lump of sugar from the bowl into my teacup with a spoon. "What has Dr. Siegel told you so far?"

"Well, he just said that I needed to have more tests done before he can tell me how we should treat it," she rested the cup back into its saucer.

I didn't bother asking her, Why didn't you tell me? What was she going to say? You were in a coma, You had to get better, I didn't want to worry you….. Instead, I asked, "Are you in pain?"

"No, not really. I get a twinge on my right side every now and then," she put her hand on the right side of her abdomen.

The first ray of hope, she had limited pain. Maybe the tumor hadn't advanced far.

"Does Billy know?"

"No, but now that you know, I will need to tell him."

My mother yawned. I looked up at the ticking clock, 11:55. Interrogating her further would not get me the answers I was looking for tonight. What type of tumor was it? Had it become invasive? Should she go to the city and see a specialist? I pushed away the thought I didn't want to entertain: how long does she have?

Chapter 16

HELEN

NOVEMBER 19, 1995

As much as I didn't want to tell Jill about my cancer diagnosis, I have to admit to myself that it is a relief to have it out in the open. I think to myself as I lie here in bed. I know Jill is strong, but she is still my little girl, my only little girl. I wish she had a sister to lean on in life like I have.

Jill shouldn't have to worry about me, especially right now. Even Father Peter at St. Francis couldn't answer me. "Why," I asked him, "why do all these bad things happen and why all at once!" He listened, unfazed and I realized that he clearly had been in this predicament before.

"One of the big mysteries of life, Helen." He then gave me his scripted response. "Being people of faith, as we are, we believe God has a plan in all of these unfortunate circumstances."

I tried to be grateful and accepting of his answer, I really did. But really, what did he know? He didn't have any kids.

"Would you like me to include you and Jill in our prayer list during Sunday mass?"

The power of prayer; I did believe in that. I thought about it. "Please include Jill in the prayer list, not me. I haven't told the kids yet. I don't want them to find out from one of the parishioners."

"OK, Helen, I will do that. I'll include a prayer for you in my silent prayers."

He was a sweet man, really. He tried. "Thank you, I appreciate that, I really do." And I meant it.

Father Peter has been a major part of our family's spiritual life. He came as a young novice priest to our parish in his twenties. He followed Monsignor John around like a puppy dog for years until Monsignor John died suddenly from a stroke on Saint Valentine's day. Father Peter was promoted and due to the decrease in young men entering the priesthood, never got a second in command to help him. No, he carried our parish alone with supporting priests from local parishes rotating in to help or give him a much-needed vacation at times. The constant requests and responsibility clearly aged him before his time.

"I don't understand, why don't they let priests date or get married? No wonder they are having trouble recruiting them." Billy said one day after mass when he was a teenager. "Who would want to sign up for that?"

William and I tried not to let Billy see us stifling a chuckle in the front seat of the car as we left mass that morning. William had promised me he had "the talk" with Billy as I did when Jill hit that tender age. The thrill of seeing the kids develop their own sense of self confidence was exciting and agonizing at the same time. They were so self-assured, thought they knew everything. Yet, at the same time clueless on what they didn't know. We could only pray they would not encounter the negative things in life, because God knows, they wouldn't listen to our warnings.

So here I thought we made it through the kids' teen

years, and we were home free, essentially unscathed only to have this terrible accident happen to Jill. It was only last year that I really let myself fall asleep, not worrying if they were out late driving. I know the broken bones are going to be the least of Jill's worries in the coming months. That orphaned little girl will haunt her, I know, in fact that will haunt all of us. I know better than to ask why. It's like a dog chasing its own tail, round and round, endlessly. I know I will never get an answer that allows it all make sense. I've been down this road before. With Father Peter's help, I've learned it's best to pray to be part of the healing, the solution or purpose God has for us all. That lesson didn't come easy. I spent months paralyzed in a body that could move perfectly fine, searching for an answer. I pray now that Jill will find an answer or direction that brings her peace and that little baby has the love and support she needs.

As exhausted as I feel, I cannot fall asleep. This evening's events have me too stirred up. I reach for my leather journal that I keep tucked under my Bible on the bottom shelf of my bedside table and retrieve a pen from the drawer. Perhaps, if I get some of these thoughts out of my head, I will be able to get some rest.

Chapter 17

JILL

NOVEMBER 21, 1995 MORNING

Sitting in Dr. Siegel's waiting room was unnerving. Luckily, my mother kept herself preoccupied leafing through the magazines that were stacked on each end table. The green carpet matched the color of the leaves in the oil paintings depicting wooded landscapes. I could hear the receptionist clicking her gum when she left the glass sliding door open after talking to a patient. It was grating on my already raw nerves.

"You can take a seat Mr. Gill, the doctor will be with you shortly." The secretary slid the glass door closed. Relief.

I knew Dr. Siegel from the hospital. He is a very good internist. I recommended my mother use him after her primary care doctor of 20 years retired. But knowing him as a colleague versus now sitting here, as a patient's family member, was very different.

"Helen Bradley" the nurse called us back while she held the doorway to the exam rooms open with her clog wearing foot. She wore a traditional white nurse's uniform, minus the old school cap, a long forgotten tradition.

My mother and I got up in unison and followed the nurse's lead. "How are you today?"

"Not bad, it is a beautiful day outside." That's my mother, always pointing out the bright side of life. I stayed silent, reserving my energy for the line of questioning stacked up in my head.

"Yes, it is amazing today, isn't it?" the nurse agreed and ushered us into exam room 2. I hobbled with my walker towards the lone chair in the room. "Please change into this gown and the doctor will be right with you." She left the gown on the exam table and closed the door behind her.

Am I supposed to help my mother change? This was very awkward. I haven't seen her naked since I was a little kid and she had no choice but to keep Billy and me with her in the bathroom with her while she showered so we wouldn't get into trouble. Gosh, where did that memory come from?

"Do you need help?" I offered.

My mother half smiled, "I think I can handle it."

"I'll wait outside, right by the door," I excused myself.

I leaned against the wallpapered cold wall. The ceramic tiled floor smelled freshly mopped with the same disinfectant the hospital used. I stared at it and counted the number of tiles in the hallway.

The exam door next to ours closed gently. I lifted my gaze and found myself staring into the eyes of Dr. Siegel. He held my gaze and I could tell that he knew that I knew of my mother's diagnosis. He lifted his left arm and motioned for me to follow him, which I did.

"I'm glad we get a chance to talk alone for a minute," he said just above a whisper as he suggested that I sit in the chair facing his desk. I followed the suggestion. "I'm really sorry, Jill. I can't imagine how tough this has all been on you." His empathy felt sincere and I willed myself not to cry.

"How bad is it?" The facts, I just needed the facts.

"We'll talk more with your mom present, but I don't have to tell you that this is a tough diagnosis."

I knew that already, I wanted him to tell me it's not that bad, he found a new treatment, it will be rough, but she'll come out fine. "I can take her to a hospital in the city, give her IV's at home, whatever she needs I can do it!" I offered.

"It's stage IV, Jill." Check mate.

Stage IV, the worst possible stage. The tumor had invaded more than the pancreas; it had probably spread all over her body. It was a wonder she was walking. Dr. Siegel looked at me and waited while I pondered my next move, even though I knew the game was over.

"But what about these new 'alternative treatments'? There must be some type of herb or cleansing or something?" I wasn't giving in without a fight.

"Jill, I'm really sorry. I have explored what I think is every option and none of them is going to get the outcome that we all want." He was killing me.

The clock on the table behind him ticked rhythmically. It sat next to a portrait of three smiling teenagers. Three. We were supposed to be three, three siblings, but it's just me and Billy. If we were three now, maybe I wouldn't be sitting here alone with my mother.

"How long does she have?"

"If you want the scientific data answer, two, maybe up to six months. But, Jill, the real answer is that we just don't know, time will tell. If I may, I'd like to share some advice, as a colleague."

Two, maybe six months was still ringing in my head, while I tried to listen to what he was offering. Christmas, maybe Easter. We have to make it through Christmas!

"When my mother had cancer, I spent every waking second trying to find a cure for her. I lost valuable time searching the library, making phone calls, scheduling

appointments with specialists, all to no avail. I fully understand that you want to help her, save her. I get that. But, Jill, right now she needs you to be her daughter, not her nurse."

Be her daughter, not her nurse. How was I going to be able to do that if I can't find the off button?

Chapter 18

HELEN

NOVEMBER 21, 1995 EVENING

"The news today wasn't good," I tell my husband when we are alone in our bedroom.

He sits on the edge of the bed next to me looking stunned. I reach out to hold his hand. For the third time, in all our years of marriage, I see him cry. Clearly his feelings must have really been bottled up, because the tears were coming out in buckets. I yearn for comfort myself, but comfort him instead.

"I can't live without you!" between sniffles.

"You will all be OK," I assure him as we grip each other's hands.

After what seems like hours of deep conversation, and nearly a whole box of Kleenex, there is no more to say, at least for now. William climbs into bed with me and holds me. It has been weeks since we were together. Thankfully, God spares me a night of nausea and we sleep without moving an inch.

Chapter 19

JILL
THANKSGIVING, NOVEMBER 23, 1995

I awoke to the whiff of basting turkey and the sound of announcers talking about this years Macy's Day Parade floats on TV. How did I sleep so late? I meant to get up early and help my mother.

I flung my casted leg off the bed, sat up and stretched like a cat. Only more week with that stupid dead weight on my leg and then I was able to ditch that walker. Even my right clavicle wasn't hurting that much anymore.

I pulled my dad's old Irish knit sweater over my flannel pajamas, slipped on my slippers and headed for the kitchen. As I got closer I could hear Billy's voice. It was really heartwarming to be all together under one roof again. I was so glad when Billy offered to spend the night so he could help my mom make Thanksgiving dinner. I know she would never have asked, but her eyes relaxed when he made his offer and she didn't fight it.

"Hey, you guys started without me?" I jested as I shuffled into the warm, fragrant kitchen.

"If we waited for you, we would be having the Thanksgiving feast for breakfast tomorrow!" Billy threw back at me while he stood at the counter shaving a head of cabbage on the large wooden cutting board.

"Wow! You're making the coleslaw?" I marveled at

Billy's culinary finesse.

"Don't look so surprised, I do live alone you know. And I certainly don't look like I am starving do I?" he pulled away from the counter and opened his arms so I could inspect his body. He certainly didn't look nutritionally depleted. In fact he looked like he was in great shape. I never really stopped to see that my little brother was really becoming a man.

Mom bent over with her head nearly in the oven as she inspected the star of today's show. "How are you feeling today, Mom? Do you want me to watch the turkey?" I offered, although I wasn't quite sure how I would balance to do it.

"I'm feeling pretty good today," she said in her upbeat tone. "Thank you, no, I am going to handle the bird today. Your father said he will take it out when it's ready and do the carving." Dad must be in the living room reading the paper.

"No turkey trot today?" I asked, just realizing it was usually just us gals in the kitchen Thanksgiving morning.

"Nah, we may do some trotting tomorrow instead, burn off all that we pack on today." Billy was now shredding carrots for the slaw.

I fumbled my way along and gathered a mug, poured some coffee, black and sat at the kitchen table filled with serving dishes and bowls waiting to be filled. Although worry and sadness threatened to invade the Rockwell moment, I willed myself to enjoy it. I made a pact with myself that I would enjoy this day, a gift that for years I just took for granted.

Chapter 20

HELEN

THANKSGIVING , NOVEMBER 23, 1995

I feel surprisingly well today, better than I have in weeks. I can't help but wonder if having the kids home again is the antidote I need. Even they look a little calmer today. Poor Billy, he looked catatonic when I first told him about my illness. Today, however, he has an extra spring in his step. I must admit, I didn't know he was such a whiz in the kitchen. He certainly never showed that side of himself when he lived here before!

I love watching the kids banter back and forth, the way siblings do. They have a way of knowing just where to jab each other and how much each other can take. God forbid someone else take a shot at them, however. When one of Jill's high school friends made a crack about Billy's souped up car, Jill shot her a look that made it clear that only she could deal a low blow like that.

I got an extra large bird this year, as large as I could get and yet still fit in my roasting pan. It is a fresh kill, not frozen like I usually get. It cost more, but this is a special Thanksgiving. I open the oven, remove the cover and baste it one more time. The turkey juice drips over the bare skin bird and dribbles into the stuffing seeping out of the inside. Soon I will leave the cover off and let the skin turn a golden crispy brown.

I reach in the freezer and pull out two bags of frozen corn and peas. I opted to take the easy way out on the extra vegetables this year not knowing how much energy I would have. I lay them on the counter near the stove and gather two pots to heat them up with when my sister arrives. We'll eat soon after she and her family arrives, so then we can just relax around the fireplace, maybe play some games, watch football, reminisce.

"Happy Thanksgiving!!" I hear coming from the front door.

"Hi Aunt Terri," Jill welcomes her.

Before I join them, I return to the turkey, remove the lid, baste it one more time.

"Happy Thanksgiving!" I greet my sister, and give her, her husband, Edgar, and three teenagers: Alex, 18, Tara, 16 and Walter, 12, named after my grandfather, with a big, warm hug each.

"May I take your coats?" Billy offers with his arm extended. What a fine young man he has turned into.

One by one they peel their wool peacoats or puffy down jackets off and Billy brings them upstairs to lie on his bed.

"It smells delicious!" Edgar exclaims.

"Thank you, I have had some wonderful help in the kitchen this year," I answer.

"Please come in, sit down. Would anyone like a drink?" William welcomes them into the living room.

"Would love one," Edgar replies. "Got any scotch and some rocks?"

"Fine choice," William agrees. "I think I will join you." William retreats to the small butler's pantry between the living room and dining room. It is lightly stocked with liquor, only the best.

"None for me, right now, thank you," Terri replies.

Her hands are full with bags and a big bowl of mashed potatoes in a white ceramic bowl covered with plastic wrap.

"Come on in the kitchen and we can put that down." She follows me, while Jill catches up with the kids in the living room.

"Are you OK?" Terri whispers to me when we are alone in the kitchen, her face looking worried.

"Surprisingly, yes, I actually feel pretty good today!" I take the bowl from her hands and put it on the table. She puts the big bag on the chair and begins to unload the pies.

"Well, don't over do it today. And if you want me to do anything, all you need to do is ask. Do you understand me?" Terri seems to be taking over the big sister role.

"Thank you, but really I am feeling good today." And I mean it. For the first time, I actually have hope that maybe I can beat this thing.

Chapter 21

JILL

CHRISTMAS EVE, DECEMBER 24, 1995

"Remember when we used to fight over who got to put the soldier with the drum on the tree?" Billy asked as he gazed at the fully decorated tree, the biggest one that we had ever gotten, nearly hitting the ceiling of our living room. On the other side of the room a gentle fire warmed our aching souls. Billy's girlfriend sat quietly beside him on the brown leather couch.

My mother lay in a hospital bed, with her head slightly tilted up. I sat on a chair right beside her. An array of presents lay beneath the tree, not nearly as many as we were used to. The ever-present Grandfather clock chimed eight times; four more hours until Christmas.

"Hot chocolate anyone?" my father asked as he entered the room. For a man who didn't even know how to turn a stove on, he was making an effort.

"No thanks, Dad." Billy replied. "I think Mindy and I are going to go out in a bit and maybe catch a bite to eat at the diner. Do you think they are open on Christmas Eve?"

"I'm not sure, but it's probably your best shot." Dad replied.

I had given up on trying to keep everyone fed in our house. The focus now was on the vigil we were keeping with my mother, never leaving her alone now that she was in and out of consciousness. Billy probably hadn't eaten since breakfast, so I couldn't blame him for wanting to get something to fill his stomach. The talk of food seemed to awaken my hunger. I ignored it and it gave up and went away. How did we get here so fast? Wasn't it just a month ago we were all gathered in the same room, complaining about how full our bellies were, complimenting Billy on pulling off the coleslaw, and listening to our younger cousins talk about high school life?

My mother looked so good that day. She wore her favorite bronze wool dress and gold heart earrings that Dad had given her for one of their many anniversaries. She seemed to float on air; so excited to have all of us together. Everyone pitched in without her having to nag us to do it.

That exuberance lasted a few more days until she took a sharp turn, which she never bounced back from. She became more nauseous, starting vomiting regularly, and her right side starting sharply jabbing her with a pain so sudden and fierce, that she would bend over and hold her breath. Dr. Siegel tried to manage the symptoms as best he could, but within a week he strongly suggested that we consider hospice because they were the experts at managing her condition. If it weren't so agonizing watching my mother suffer so, I would have fought that recommendation and insist that we pursue aggressive treatment. But in the end, it was her decision, and as stoic as she normally was, she gave in.

Being in hospice care meant that we, and especially my mother, recognized and accepted that she was going to die and that her care would be comfort oriented, not treatment focused. Well, they can give up on her, I thought, but I'm not. I continued to scour medical journals, the Internet, talk to other cancer survivors for the treatment I knew would cure her. And I prayed, and prayed, that God would save her. When it only got worse, I began to pray that if God would not save her, he would take her to heaven and relieve her of the pain and suffering. I felt so guilty praying for that since that was a prayer not just to relieve her, but me. I didn't know how much more I could take.

Billy and Mindy got up. Billy stopped at the bed, reached down and kissed my mom on her forehead. She remained still. Then he went to the coat closet, retrieved Mindy's blue pea coat, and held it behind her while she put it on. My little bro, turning into a chivalrous gentleman, I beamed with pride.

Alone with just my parents, my dad stood at the foot of my mother's bed and gazed at her with a warm mug of something in his hands. There was no room left for conversation. What more could we say?

I too gazed over to my mother. My 45-year-old mother. Her robust body now deteriorated to a thinly skinned skeleton. Her hair, which was always permed and dyed summer blond was now cut short and matted. She was clean, however. And kept pain free, I saw to that. When the hospice team suggested that we have her transferred to an inpatient setting, I strictly objected. If I couldn't save my mother, the least I could do was keep her comfortable and let her die in her own home. The home she raised us in, she lovingly decorated and hosted parties in. I knew she wanted it that way.

"I'm going for a drive to get some fresh air, I'll be back soon." My father said. When I turned he was already headed toward the kitchen. I wondered if he was crying. There he goes again, I thought. My father had been noticeably absent these past few weeks. It seems the worse my mom got, the less we saw of him. "Everyone grieves differently," the hospice counselor told me and Billy. We'll have plenty of time to grieve if she dies, I wanted to yell, we need our dad here now. Mom needs his support.

I heard the back door slam and my dad's car back out of the driveway. "Well, it's just us gals again," I said to my mother as I gently stroked her hair. Her breathing was changing. It had been all day. Her breath quickened now, fast, short breaths. I stood up and then her breathing paused; Cheyne-Stoke respirations, a sign that the end was near. A huge lump welled up in my throat. Gingerly, I let the side rail of the bed down and climbed in beside her. Spooning her, I let my cheek rest on her boney cheek. "I love you, Mama," I squeaked out. I could swear that I saw her cheeks and lips rise into a smile, before she took her last shallow breath.

Chapter 22

HELEN

CHRISTMAS EVE, DECEMBER 24, 1995

"Welcome home!!" the crowd cheered.

The homecoming party that awaited me was unimaginable, far better than any party I had ever planned. A huge crowd of familiar faces that I had missed for years beamed smiles simultaneously at me. They all stood in the center of a grass field surrounded by fragrant wildflowers. The sky was cloudless in a shade of blue that I had never seen before. In the distance, picnic tables lined up with balloons and puffs of smoke seeped out of grills suggesting delicious treats await.

Front and center of the crowd, stood my parents, Edna and Howard. They both looked young and healthy, the way I remembered them when I was in grade school. Oh, how I had missed them so! My father had his arms outstretched wide waiting for a hug. My mother, on the other hand, held a young infant dressed in pink with white leather saddle shoes and stockings on. She turned the baby toward me and said, "Look who's here, Katie, Mommy is here!"

I ran and snatched my little girl out of my mother's arms and held her as close to me as I could. She cooed in my ear as I kissed her over and over again, not missing an inch of her face. "My baby, oh my baby!!!" Surprisingly, I didn't cry, there was only an overwhelming feeling of love and joy in my heart. Katie cooed and when I pulled her away to soak her all in, she reached up and touched my cheek with her pudgy little hand and smiled.

My mother and father wrapped their arms around both of us and we stood there in a group hug while the others waited their turn. Eventually, my parent's let go, but I would not release my baby, Kate. My favorite Aunt Sophie kissed me, as did my grandparents from both sides, while, Oscar, our big floppy sheepdog from my childhood stood at my feet.

"Suzie!" I shouted in surprise to my long lost high school friend. "I didn't know you were here!"

"Been here a while now. When they told me you were coming I said I wouldn't miss the welcome reception for the world!" She said with a glass of iced tea filled with ice in her hands.

To say it was overwhelming would be an understatement. Mr. Strauss who owned the local bakery, Uncle Tom who always took us kids to the amusement park, why, if my eyes were seeing right, I think I even saw Jesus in the background playing volleyball. While more and more people from my past came up to welcome me home, I couldn't help but want to just stand there and be with my baby. I clung on to her and marveled that she looked exactly the same as I remembered her and even smelled of the baby shampoo I used to wash her hair with. "Oh, baby, you have no idea how much I missed you!"

"It's about time you got here!" It was Dawn, my beloved friend from our Stitch and Bitch club. Dawn's hair was back to the way it was before she got cancer and she looked as robust as ever.

I paused and looked at my hands, my body and if I

could have found a mirror, I would have looked into it. My hands were no longer yellow, dry and skeleton-like. They were smooth and soft, my fingernails long and manicured, painted my favorite coral pink color.

"The best part of being here, is you return to the best self you ever were on earth!" Dawn told me as she watched my bewilderment.

As I stood amongst the joyous crowd, a feeling of something forgotten tugged at me; a feeling like a door left open that still needed to be shut. My gut knew what it was, and I knew this feeling wouldn't go away until I completed some unfinished business. Reluctantly, I found my mother and handed Katie to her. "Mother, could you hold onto Katie just a little while longer?"

My mother reached out for the baby and didn't ask why. When the baby left my arms, the entire crowd and scene swept away into a giant light. I found myself sitting in a quiet, serene, blizzard blue room with one bench, alone. In front of me was a window. I got up and went to it.

Chapter 23

JILL
DECEMBER 28, 1995

"Do you need a chair?" my father leaned over and asked me.

"No, I'm OK," I replied. My leg muscles felt tight, but they didn't hurt. I could withstand the last line of patrons coming to say goodbye. My persistence with my physical therapy plan was paying off since they removed my cast a couple of weeks ago. The last couple of days had been surprisingly emotionless. While I knew my body was present at the wake and funeral, I didn't feel like I was. I listened to several people share their sorrows and fondest memories of my mom, but only a few of them remained in my memory.

Jack, of course, was one of them. He and his parents came to the wake. If they came to the funeral, I didn't see them. We took a moment to talk alone, Jack and I, outside the funeral home.

"Hey, I can't tell you how sorry I am about all that has happened to you." He said while he kept his hands in the pockets of his blue wool pants and pretended to kick a stone or something with his left foot. "You've been through a lot. Your mom was awesome, like a second mom to me."

I didn't dare open my mouth to reply, knowing

nothing good would come out.

He continued on, clearly uncomfortable with my silence, "My mom says you have grit, you are strong, you'll pull through."

Grit, great, just what I wanted to hear. Not long legs, voluptuous flowing brown hair or big boobs, no, I have grit. Again, I bit my tongue.

"Well, listen, again, I'm really sorry about all that's going on, I hope things get better."

"Thanks," was the only thing that I could think to say that I wouldn't regret later.

Becky came up to me when she saw Jack leave. "How did that go?"

"Cold, uncomfortable." The only way I could describe it.

Becky came to all of the functions, the wake, the funeral, and the final gathering in the church's reception hall. She was always close by, just in case I needed something.

When most of the people had cleared out of the church reception area, Becky looked around, "Do you want to come and stay over at my place tonight?"

As nice as the thought of getting out of my parents' house was, I was hesitant because of my dad. "I don't want to leave my dad alone just yet."

"What did you say about your dad?" my father said from behind me.

"Becky invited me up to her place tonight, but I told her I didn't want to leave you alone just yet."

"Nonsense, you should go," he said, way too easily. "A girls' night will do you a world of good."

Reluctantly, I agreed. "OK, it won't be until later tonight though. We have to go to the cemetery and then I have to go home and get some things."

"That's fine. You take your time. Whenever you get to my place, we'll order pizza and just chill." Becky gave me a big southern hug and then headed out.

***

My dad, brother and I chose to have the burial in private. We only invited Mom's sister and her family to join us. We each placed a sunny yellow sunflower, Mom's favorite, on her polished mahogany casket. The gravediggers had already dug the 6-foot hole, which I found to be very morbid. I waited in the car while they actually lowered her in; that was not the last memory I wanted to hold onto of her.

We drove home in silence. Still stunned. We dropped Billy off at his place, and Dad and I went home. It felt foreign to go into our home without Mom in it. I suspected my dad felt that too, because he immediately said, "I've got to run out and do a few things. I may not see you before you leave for Becky's, so have a good time and drive safe." He didn't even come into the house. He tipped the limo driver and got right into his car.

I entered the house alone, greeted only by the hum of the refrigerator and the ticking of the grandfather clock in the distance. I put my black clutch down on the kitchen table. There was no point in sitting down, when there was no one there to talk to. I walked over to the stove and touched the handle to the green kettle. How could someone be here one minute and then gone the next? As much as I thought I had prepared myself for my mother's death, I realized there was no way to prepare. How can you prepare to have a life without someone whom you have always had in yours?

I wandered aimlessly, room to room, somehow

thinking I would find her, ready to greet me cheerfully as she always did. No matter where I searched, she wasn't there. I entered her bedroom and sat down on her side of the antique sleigh bed with the handmade quilt. Her Bible sat on the shelf of her bedside table. I reached for it and held it close to my chest. I lay down in the bed and opened the book. "To our daughter who we love, may the Lord bless you always," was inscribed on the inside signed, "With Love, Mother and Papa." Again, I held it close to my chest, like it was she herself. I would keep this. My father and brother would never know it was missing. They probably didn't even know it existed.

As I lie there and let my mind try to soak in all that had transpired, I looked down again at the shelf of the end table. There was another book there, with a grainy leather cover. I reached over and pulled it up onto the bed with me as well. As I leaned up on my elbow with my right hand holding up my head, I opened this newfound treasure with my left.

October 15,1995: I've never written in a journal before. An article in this month's Ladies Home Journal said it is a healthy way to process your thoughts, find answers to problems, discover new truths about yourself, document your past. I'm not sure what to write, exactly but I am going to give it a whirl.

A journal! I found my mother's journal! I never knew she kept one. It was the first feeling of excitement I felt in months. I sat up and gathered the books and headed into my bedroom. As I did this, I noticed snow was dancing past the windows. I didn't know they were calling for snow. It was sticking already. I reached for the phone and dialed Becky's number.

"Hello," Becky answered.

"Hey, Becky, it's me. Listen, it looks like it's getting slippery out there with this snow. Can I just come tomorrow instead?" I kept the journal discovery to myself.

"Sure, honey, that's fine. It's probably a good idea. I just saw on the news it may accumulate to a few inches, surprise storm coming through. I am off tomorrow, so just give me a call when you leave your house."

"OK, I will, thanks, Beck," I replaced the phone, then hung my black sweater dress up in the closet and peeled off my stockings. My two-piece flannel PJ's were a welcome retreat. I was actually looking forward to my evening. I just wanted to curl up in my bed and read my mother's journal. What stories would she tell? What secrets might I discover? Did she leave any messages, final words of wisdom?

Chapter 24

HELEN

DECEMBER 28, 1995

"Yeah!! You found my journal!" I cheered, as I stood alone in the tranquil blue room, watching Jill out of the lone window. I wished now that I had started a journal earlier or shared more with my daughter. Things just always seemed to be so busy, meals to cook, school work to get done, parties to plan. Before I knew it, Jill was off to college and never came back. By the time she did come back, I felt so sick; I could barely keep my thoughts straight, never mind have a conversation.

Looking back, though, perhaps she was better off not knowing everything, hearing all my advice. She'll learn that now. I look over her shoulder to see what page she is on.

October 15, 1995: It broke my heart to watch William's reaction to my diagnosis today. I know he loves me and I him. After so many years together, we can speak without saying a word, laugh just by looking at something the same way. Sure, we've had our disagreements, but we've learned that fighting never gets us to where we want to be. Perhaps that all comes with wisdom and aging, or that the stress in our lives at this point is generally less. Well, at least it was, until now.

I watch Jill lay the journal down flat on the pages. Her eyes were getting heavy. I can feel her thinking, "My poor parents, they had only received this news just a few days before my accident."

Please, honey, don't shoulder all this guilt! It was not your fault. It was mine. Keep reading, you will understand why. I willed her to hear me. But Jill's exhaustion took over and I watched her fall into a much-needed deep sleep.

Chapter 25

JILL

DECEMBER 29, 1995

The sound of the snow shovel scraping the driveway jolted my eyes open. My mother's journal jabbed into my rib. As much as I wanted to jump right back into it, I realized that it was probably my father out there shoveling. The last thing I needed was for him to have a heart attack.

I got out of bed, stretched and looked out the window. Yup, Dad was out there, shoveling away. It looked like we only got a couple of inches, but I thought it better if I called the O'Brien brothers next door to see if they wanted to make some quick cash. It's hard to believe they are teenagers now, wasn't it just yesterday I was babysitting them? I wrapped my bathrobe around me, slipped into my slippers and headed downstairs to retrieve my father.

As I meandered down the stairs the smell of pancakes and bacon made me pause. Did Dad actually get up this morning and make himself a full breakfast? He probably wasn't even aware that I was home. My parents had insisted that I park my car in the garage while they parked theirs in the driveway since I came back here. I meant to leave him a note last night, but I fell fast asleep before doing so. I rubbed my eyes and continued down the stairs. The clank of a pan against the sink made me stop again. Billy? Did Billy come over to cook Dad breakfast? I quickened my step, and headed for the kitchen.

"You're just in time, I've made your favorite breakfast!" A woman, whom I had never seen before, stood at the sink wearing a knee high silk black bathrobe and satin slippers.

She turned and I'm not sure who had the more shocked look on their face, her or me.

"Oh!" was all she could say.

I didn't bother asking who she was. I marched straight past her and headed out the back door. The shoveled steps had a thin layer of ice and threatened to throw me down, but I grabbed onto the railings for dear life, steadied myself, and then continued in search of my father.

Hearing the crunch of the hardened snow under my feet, my father stood straight up, shovel in hand, and turned around. Again a look of shock, this time his more than mine. Mine reeked of poison darts .

"Who is that woman in our kitchen?" I demanded.

"Jill, I can explain," he tried, as he wiped his dripping nose with his sleeve.

"Explain, there is nothing to explain! Who is she?" Vapor poured out of my mouth like a smokestack. The heat from my rage protected me from the below freezing temperature.

"Her name is Marian." He wasn't even going to get in the ring to fight. He already gave up.

"You mean to tell me you couldn't even wait until my mother, your wife, of how many years, was put in her final resting place before you took up with someone else?" I didn't wait for a reply. I turned around and stormed back inside. Let him have a heart attack. Miss Silky Robe was gone, probably went upstairs to put something decent on. A full stack of pancakes, with a side plate of bacon, sat on the table with two place settings. I took the two plates and threw them against the wall. The plates shattered; I didn't wait to see where it all landed.

Flames roared inside of me. I bolted up to my room. I changed, grabbed my duffle bag that was packed from the night before and threw my mother's journal in it.

Downstairs, I found my black clutch, threw on my winter coat and boots, and headed for the garage. As I backed out I noticed my father was nowhere to be found. Coward! I plowed through the half shoveled driveway even though the car tried to squirm off onto the lawn. I headed to my brother's house while the potent sunrise blinded me. Hootie and the Blowfish's song, "Let Her Go," crooned on the radio. "Let her go, Let her walk right out on me." That's right, I'm walking out on you, Dad. I switched it off and rode in silence.

My poor mother, I thought to myself, as I drove along. Did she know? It was all making sense now, the footsteps to his office, which never returned to the bedroom. No wonder he encouraged me to go to Becky's last night. My mind continued to back track and put the pieces of the puzzle together. The glistening trees and kids having snowball fights tried to brighten my spirits, but I was in no mood.

I made it up the steep shared driveway to the front of Billy's house and took the short walkway to the front door. I knew he didn't fix the doorbell yet, so I just pounded on the door. Billy opened it rather quickly and stood there. I've seen Billy's look of fear after being caught buying a motorcycle and hiding it from my parents, sneaking girlfriends into the basement and once trying marijuana, but this look took the cake.

"You knew, didn't you!" I screamed. Obviously, Dad had called him to warn him that I might be headed his way.

"Jill, come inside, let's talk about this," he looked at me, then peeked out the door to see if I had stirred any of his neighbors.

"I don't need to talk about this! He couldn't keep his dick in his pants until my mother was at least in her grave?" I continued to shout.

"Jill, this has been hard on everyone. He's a guy…"

Well, that was the last straw! "He's a guy! That's going to be the excuse?" I turned around, and stomped back to my car. I was out of here, to where I didn't know, but away from here.

Grinding my teeth, I drove through the center of Nyack while I formulated my next move. The light on the corner of Maple and Main turned red. To my left was the travel agency the same one that my mom used to book our beach vacations. Posters of exotic places filled the windows. The one with "Escape to Paradise" with a backdrop of a beach with Caribbean blue water caught my eye. I pulled the car over and parked leaving the passenger side tires propped up on the plowed ice. Go ahead, let them give me a ticket, I don't have time to put money in the meter, I said to myself as I headed for the agency. As I got closer to the poster I had my eye on, I noticed the slogan on the bottom, "Heaven on Earth." I was certainly willing to find out what that means, because right now, my life sucked!

A bell rang when I entered the travel agency. Although there were several desks lined up back to back, only one had an agent sitting at it. Marge Crumb was inscribed on the nameplate that sat in front of her desk.

Marge pulled her glasses halfway down her nose and looked up at me, "May I help you?"

"Good morning, yes. Where is that place that is depicted in that poster?" I pointed to the one in the front window.

"That is the island of Triton. It is a very small island. They just started promoting tourism. They run a chartered flight out of JFK twice a week. I haven't been there myself, but the few people who have gone really loved it!"

"When is the next flight?" I asked.

Marge pulled out her file drawer, took a minute to find what she was looking for, leafed through it, then replied, "This afternoon, at 5 pm, the next one isn't until next week, Tuesday".

"I'd like to book a trip there over New Year's. Can I get on today's 5 pm flight?"

Marge looked at me quizzically, but she wasn't going to argue with a sure commission. "If you would like to take a seat, I will make a couple of phone calls and make sure there is a seat and room at the resort, Sea and Sand. It is an all inclusive and the only one on the island. It would be your best bet. There are only a few other mom and pop type hotels, but they are a bit iffy."

I sat down, "That would be fine."

As I sat and waited, Marge made her calls and scribbled notes on a pad. Occasionally she paused, put her hand on the receiver and asked me a question, "Oceanfront room or garden view?"

"Oceanfront." What the hell, I may as well splurge; make the best of this escape.

I made a mental note to myself, go to the bank, and get travelers checks. My disability checks and savings from not paying rent should have added to my already descent size savings. Right after college graduation I began an aggressive savings campaign, thinking I would need it for my future with Jack. Luckily, my mother had made me get a safe deposit box to put my birth certificate, my passport and some stock certificates in, so I wouldn't need to go back to the house for those. My passport only had one stamp in it, from Greece, where we took our last family trip, a cruise, when my brother moved out. I would stop at the mall, pick up a suitcase and some clothes, a bathing suit and flip flops, and maybe grab a book to read.

"OK, you are all set. How would you like to pay for this?"

I fished in my pocketbook for my credit card and handed it to her. She completed the necessary transaction, finished up the paperwork and handed me a tropical folder. "This is your plane ticket. This is your transfer voucher to the hotel; a bus will be waiting at the airport with the resort name on the side. This is your confirmation for the hotel. Will that be all?"

I stood up and reached to shake Marge's hand. "Yes, thank you."

"You sure are in a hurry to go on vacation," Marge commented. Concerned or just being nosy, I wasn't quite sure. Either way, I didn't want to go into it.

I just nodded, "Thank you, again."

Back in my car, I took a moment. The snow that blanketed the sidewalks was now turning to slush as the sun strengthened. Am I crazy? Did I just book a trip to somewhere that I have never even heard of, all by myself? Before I talked myself out of it, I turned the key and headed for the bank.

Chapter 26

HELEN

DECEMBER 29, 1995

I watched as Marian sat on the edge of my bed trying to console William who clearly was upset. I had suspected that something was going on with him soon after we got my cancer diagnosis. He was devastated, "What am I going to do, I can't live without you!"

He never held me the same after that, barely came near me, like the cancer was contagious. It was deeply hurtful, but not surprising. I had come to learn that while William was a very strong leader in business, he was weak in matters of the home. If I had possessed more energy, I would have tried to support him better, fight for him, but it was all I could do to get my daily functions done. Add to that, Jill's accident and then all that ensued from it. William couldn't function without a sturdy anchor to keep him from being pulled out to sea when the tides of life stirred up.

My Billy, such a kind-hearted soul, always seemed to get caught in the crossfire. He drove over to Mindy's apartment after Jill left his house. She was good for him, I was grateful he found her.

My men, they would be OK. It was Jill, whom I was more concerned about. I have to admit that I was kind of proud that she gave them both a what for. I wish I had

had the strength to do that! She has always been stronger, more tenacious than me. I noticed it early on, when we gave her a make believe kitchen set for her fourth birthday. William and I set the mini oven, not much higher than her up in the living room, on Christmas Eve after the kids had gone to bed. It came with a frying pan, bread pan, and two small pots to work with. I sewed her an apron, just like the one that I wore, and she wore it with great pride as she made her favorite dishes.

"Mom, I need water in my pot to boil eggs," Jill announced one day, while I was preparing supper in the kitchen. She held her small pot out to me.

I pretended to pour water in it, but that didn't satisfy her. "No, Mom, I need real water."

"Baby, I don't want you cooking with real water in my living room. This will have to do," again, I simulated pouring water in her bowl. "Now go on, boil your eggs, I have to baste the chicken."

She trudged out of the kitchen with a scowl on her face. After I finished preparing supper for the evening, I went to check up on the kids. As I neared the living room, I could hear Jill humming to herself, "La, de, da," and the sound of stirring. I tiptoed to the living room entry and peered around the corner. Jill stood at her stove, her back to me, singing and stirring. I marveled at how much she resembled me at the stove. Then, I noticed her take her pot off the imaginary burner and pour liquid into a small bowl.

"Jill, where did you get that water?" I interrupted.

Without an ounce of guilt for disobeying me, she replied, "Mom, that isn't water, I peed in the pot."

That was just the beginning. I learned my Jill was clever, smart, caring, courageous, determined—I could go on and on. But under her skin, that appeared impenetrable, I knew she had a soft heart. She was the one I still worried about. She is the one I needed to keep an eye on.

Chapter 27

JILL
DECEMBER 29, 1995

"Are you sure about this?" Becky asked with heavy concern. "Why don't you just come over here to my place, and we'll talk about this some more."

"I appreciate you offering to help. Becky, I'm tired of talking. I've been talking to that psychiatrist, talking to Marie, to you…I need a break. Maybe a total change of atmosphere will help clear my head."

"Well, OK, but what about your dad and brother? They're going to worry."

I hesitated. Let them worry is what I wanted to say. "Can you call my brother for me and just tell him that I'm OK, that I'm taking some time for myself."

"Sure, but you know, they are going to want to know where you are, "Becky replied.

"You will know what to say," and I knew Becky would. It was a lot to dump in her lap. I would find a way to pay her back later.

"We are now boarding Flight 1157 to Triton Island," the woman behind the podium said via the loud speaker. "Please have your boarding passes out and begin boarding at Gate 3."

"My flight is boarding, I've got to go," I said.

"Well…." Becky wasn't convinced she should let me

go off like this, I knew she wasn't.

For a moment, I second-guessed myself. Too exhausted to come up with an alternate solution to today's drama, I said, "I'll try to call you. If not, I will call as soon as I get back."

"Now boarding flight 1157 to Triton Island, Gate 3," the attendant repeated.

I didn't wait for Becky to talk me out of my trip. I hung up the phone and headed for the gate.

"Seat 10A, have a nice flight," the attendant wearing a dark blue blazer with wings on the lapel said as she handed me my half of the boarding pass.

I boarded the plane, looking forward to seeing what "Heaven on Earth" was like.

Chapter 28

HELEN

DECEMBER 29, 1995

I sat in the empty seat next to Jill. I really wished that Becky could have talked her out of the crazy idea to take this trip. Who ever heard of Triton Island?

"Please pull the emergency card out of the pocket in the seat in front of you. We are going to review the emergency procedures."

I only see Jill and the woman sitting in the aisle seat two rows ahead of us, the one with rosary beads in her hands, pull out the card. I scanned the half filled plane. Outdoorsy looking couples reading diving magazines, a few scattered single people, and a couple looking romantically at each other sat across the aisle.

"If anyone has any questions, please ask your flight attendants as they pass through the aisle." A middle aged woman, wearing too much rouge, sauntered down the aisle looking side to side.

I watched as Jill returned the emergency card to the seat pocket and pulled out the in flight magazine. The front cover featured a picture of a large shell twisted like a soft ice cream cone with a large opening at the base. The kind that you hold up to your ear and listen to the sound of the sea. The color of the shell was a pattern I had never seen before. Its vanilla-white coated base, had at least six different shades of brown ranging from soft tan to dark chocolate woven into each row of swirl. The very point of the shell seemed to blend all the colors together to form a shade of nude skin peach. Triton Festival in bold letters was written along the bottom of the cover.

Jill flipped through the magazine to the page featuring the festival. We read about it together.

An annual tradition, Triton Island celebrates the start of each New Year honoring its namesake, the Triton shell. The locals believe that the Triton shell is the male version of the conch shell while the Queen conch is the female. Greek mythology talks of a Greek god called Triton, the messenger of the sea. He is depicted as a merman, the top half of his body man with barnacled seashell shoulders, his bottom half the tail of a fish. Triton used the twisted triton conch shell as a trumpet, which was said to give him power to calm and raise the waves. The annual Triton festival is a way of patronizing Triton in the hopes that he would keep the local tides balanced, free of tidal waves, tsunamis or hurricanes.

"Would you like something to drink?" the flight attendant asked Jill.

"Just a water will be fine, thank you."

Jill closed the magazine and put it back in the seat pocket. She took the water and sipped it as she looked out the window. The early darkness that coincided with the recent winter solstice blocked any potential view.

With just ice cubes left in her glass, Jill bent over and fetched my journal out of her backpack. I had hoped that she would not resume reading it until she was somewhere comfortable and alone. The part that I needed her to read was just two pages away from where she left off. I had no idea how she would react. Fear that she would be angry with me or worse, hate me, kept me from telling her myself while I was on earth.

She opened the leather bound book and removed the piece of Kleenex box she had torn off to make a makeshift bookmark.

The most unbearable part of this cancer diagnosis is the thought of dying. I am not afraid of death. I have faith that I will not just drop off the face of the earth, but rather transform. Transform into what, I am not sure, but something else. I believe that I will indeed go somewhere beautiful, peaceful.

No, my biggest worry is for my family, especially my kids. I know what it is like to lose a mother. My own mother died at the age of thirty-nine, when I was just twenty years old. I was very blessed that she saw William and me get married. Just two months later, however, she was diagnosed with breast cancer. Three months after that she was gone.

Although I had my mother-in-law to lean on and help guide me when I became a mother myself, it wasn't the same. I wanted to ask my own mother so many questions; why did she choose to bottle feed us, did she think boys should be raised differently from girls, how did she treat our diaper rash, the list never ended. I envied my peers who also were having children at the same time. Their moms were excited to be grandmothers for the most part. They had instant babysitters available. I, on the other hand, always felt like I was intruding on William's mother if I needed help. In retrospect, she probably wished that I called more often than I did. She loved the kids and they loved her.

The kids were so cute when they were little! William and I used to love to take them to Jones Beach. We would get up early and I would make sandwiches out of fresh cold cuts. Jill loved turkey with mayo, while Billy loved ham with mustard. They both would insist that the crust be cut off.

I would pack the cooler while William loaded the station wagon with our beach gear; beach chairs, buckets, shovels, towels and a large old quilt. Once we had ourselves organized and suited up, we would wake up the kids for the hour-long ride. Jill loved her pink bathing suit that had a giant purple daisy on the front and a frilly skirt along the midline. She wore it so often the bottom eventually eroded to the point you could see her tushy. It was one of the few times I was actually grateful that Billy teased her.

"Your hiney is showing!" He would yell and point to her behind. His continual taunting eventually made her give in and wear the new suit that had been waiting for her for weeks.

Our voyage would begin by riding over the Tappan Zee Bridge heading towards Long Island. It always reminded me that we lived in such an geographically desirable location. From the midpoint of the bridge I would marvel at the view of New York City; the Twin Towers, and the Empire State Building, standing taller than the rest of the buildings. In just an hour drive we would be at one of the longest, cleanest beaches I know of. If we chose to go two hours west instead, as we did in the fall and winter, we were amongst farms and mountains.

When we arrived at Jones Beach park, we always tried to get into Field 6. Only the early birds got into

Field 6 on a perfect sunny day. It had the shortest walk from the parking lot to the actual beach and a reasonable walk across the sand to the ocean. It was all William and I could do to contain the kids while he and I loaded up like donkeys and made our way through the sand to find a place to sit. It was all worth it, though, once we established camp around the rented yellow umbrella. All of the stress, worries, and preoccupied thoughts seemed to dissipate from both of us. We could focus on just "being" with our children and having fun.

I watch as Jill let the journal rest in her lap. She turned and looked out the window and puts her hand on her heart.

Chapter 29

JILL

DECEMBER 29, 1995

Ahh, Jones Beach, so many memories! Billy and I loved to go there! We would always take my moms big station wagon, the one with three rows of seats and faux wood paneling on the side.

In our early years, Billy and I would ride in the middle seat together. In our teen years, however, we would fight over who got the very back seat.

Sometimes my mother would let us each choose a friend to bring with us. I would always choose Sandy, while Billy would typically pick Sandy's brother, Jim. They lived just a few houses away, so they were very close friends growing up. After they moved away in high school, we tried to stay friends as pen pals, but eventually we lost touch.

Sandy and I would sneak out our *Teen Times* magazine when it was our turn in the back seat. I had a huge crush on Scott Baio, who played as The Fonz's younger cousin, Chachi, on *Happy Days*. Luckily, Sandy had a crush on someone else. She loved rock star Bruce Springsteen. We would cut the pictures out of our loves until the only pages left were of ads and pictures of guys we weren't particularly interested in.

If the song "Dancing in the Dark" came on during

the ride, Sandy would plaster her ear to the back speaker and insist that I not say anything during the song. Billy and Jim always found out what were up to and they would mock us, "Oh, Scott, Oh, Bruce!! Smooch, Smooch, Smooch!!"

I couldn't tell you what roads we took to get to Jones Beach, but we always knew we were getting close when we saw the guardrails and light posts along the middle of the highway turn from steel to brown wood.

"We're almost there!" we would scream.

My mother would always turn around and confirm, "Almost!"

The entrance to Field 6 was labeled with a sign made of the same wooden material as the guardrails. Under it there was a sign that warned, "No Dogs Allowed," with a picture of a dog and a big red X over it. Billy and I would poise, ready for action, as we waited to catch the very first glimpse of the sign. When we did, it was a race to see who could scream out first, "Jill (or Billy), you have to get out of the car! No dogs allowed!"

I don't remember much about setting up our beach area. That was probably because Billy and I would tear off our clothes, then race to the water's edge to see what temperature it was, which was always pretty cold! We were only allowed to go in to our knees until my parents joined us. While we waited, I would stand mesmerized by the sensation of moving, without actually doing so, when the waves would retreat out to sea around my feet.

My mom and I would take our time acclimating to the cold Atlantic water. Billy and Dad, however, would run, side by side, as far as they could until they found a big wave to dive into, head on. Eventually, we'd all meet up and ride the waves together.

Despite just having had our routine breakfast cereal

with milk, we were always starving when we got out of the water! Time was irrelevant; we would eat our first batch of sandwiches by 10am. It wasn't long after that, that the vendor guys would trudge through the sand carrying Styrofoam coolers yelling, "Ice cream, chipwiches, frozen Italian ice!" My dad would give in by the third pass and hand us each a dollar.

Things became a lot different when my sister, Baby Kate, came around. Up until then, our family was evenly matched. When Kate came, things seemed unbalanced, I realize now as I look back. Days at the beach weren't the same. "You go in with your Dad, Jill, I'm going to stay here under the umbrella and feed Kate."

Dad would do his best to appease Billy and me. He'd grab us both by the hand and we'd all jump in together. But Billy always wanted to go out deeper than I did. He whined that I took too long to get into the water. Dad always waited for me.

When Kate grew old enough to walk, I enjoyed trying to teach her how to build a sand castle. She'd sit next to me and watch, but she was always more interested in seeing what sand tasted like.

The stewardess interrupted my flashback. "Tonight we are serving meatloaf with mashed potatoes and gravy or fried chicken with French fries, which would you like?" Her exuberance was overkill for the frozen dinner meals she was offering.

"I'll try the meatloaf, thank you." I pulled down the tray table in front of me, while she peeled the foil off my meal and then placed it on the tray. "Thank you."

Alone with my thoughts again, I retraced my steps back to playing with Katie in the sand. It was a warm memory. I remember being so excited when my parents first told us that we were going to have a baby. "I hope it's a girl! I want someone to play dolls and bake with!" In my mind, the baby would come to us play ready.

My wish for a girl came true, but she was not ready to play with me. She was more like a doll herself. This wasn't so bad in the beginning; I enjoyed bathing and dressing her with Mom. After a while Mom let me hold her and sometimes even feed her once her head wasn't bobbling all over the place. I remember she slept a lot, so that didn't really interrupt our routine too much. But once Baby Kate started to get teeth and walk it was a whole different story.

"No! Don't eat my Barbie," I recall yelling at Kate as she sucked on the head of my favorite Barbie doll, ruining the new hairdo I had just created on her.

"Jill, she's just a baby, please don't yell at her like that. You will have to play with your dolls in your room or at the dining room table. We don't want her to choke," mom defended her.

And so it was, our new triangle. Kate would do something that typically I didn't like and Mom would yell at me. "You're the older sister," she would say.

Our tense moments eventually intertwined with what was beginning to be play for both Kate and I. I taught her to play patty cake and we would sit on the living room floor going back and forth. Kate would giggle, drool a little, and say one of the few words she knew, "More!"

"I am going to put Kate in her rolly chair and put her on the front porch. Will you please watch her while I finish making the potatoes for dinner?" Mom asked me one afternoon.

"OK," I said, and I remembered being OK with that request.

"It's such a beautiful fall day, it is too nice to be inside, it will do you both some good to be outside for a bit," Mom said as she wheeled Kate out in her chair, more like a rolling cage, for she could not get out of it, while I held the door open. It had a flowered plastic lined cloth attached to a metal frame with wheels on it. She could choose to stand and move in it or sit and relax. A metal tray was in the front with wooden beads that could be moved around on their spool. "Close the gate on the stairs and make sure it is latched."

Our covered front porch wrapped around three quarters of the house. The only way in and out was through the front of it and that had six steep steps to it. I walked over and pulled the accordion wood gate that was already anchored to one post and latched it shut on the other.

Kate loved to play hide and go seek with me on the porch with her bear named Boo. Boo bear was a gray-brown furry bear about the size of Kate's head. His black eyes and nose were crocheted on and his mouth was done in pink. The fur was half missing from one ear because Kate had gnawed it off. I would take it from Kate and say, "Where is Boo bear?" then run and hide around one of the porch corners and poke him around the corner every now and then so she had a clue. Kate would waddle over in her rolling chair to find me. When she did, I'd yell, "Here he is!" She would reach out for him, I would let her hold him and then eventually she would hand him back to me and say, "More!"

That was the last fond memory I had of Baby Kate.

Chapter 30

HELEN

DECEMBER 29, 1995

I watched as Jill picked at her meatloaf dinner then covered it back with its foil cover leaving half of it untouched. She gazed out the plane window in thought.

"All done?" the flight attendant inquired.

"Yes, thank you," Jill handed her the leftovers, returned her tray table back to its stowed position and picked up my journal again.

Those memories of Jones Beach and time with the children are some of my most precious treasures. It seems like times were really good back then, hectic and challenging, but also fun and full of love. William and I agreed we had a very good life, two children, a boy and a girl, and that was enough for us both.

Then came our surprise, Baby Kate. Right from the start, Kate rocked our world, but we decided to stay in faith that this was God's plan for us, not our own. We pulled the crib back out of the attic, which for some reason, we never gave away. Once again, I set up a nursery in my small sewing room, packing my work away for another time. I tried to involve Jill and Billy from the start. How should we decorate the baby's room?

"With flowers!" Jill voted.

“No, dinosaurs,” retorted Billy.

Since we didn’t know the sex of the baby we added a little of both.

Jill was thrilled when the baby turned out to be a girl; Billy, not so much. William and I were just grateful she was a healthy, six-pound, seven-ounce baby. She turned out to be a very good baby, too, and I thanked God every day for that. She didn’t fuss much, and slept through the night quicker than the first two did. The stress that came with new motherhood was replaced with stress on how to care for everyone’s needs now that William and I were outnumbered. Our three-ring circus only got harder to juggle, as they got older. It still makes me clench my jaw when I think back to that time period.

The ‘if onlies’ began to creep in. If only…If only I had asked William’s mother for more help, if only I had said “yes” when my husband suggested that maybe we hire a babysitter to help out, if only I had let Jill go over to Sandy’s that day when she was invited. Jill was always such a mature little girl; I grew to lean on her, my little mother. I know I put too much burden on her, it is still the greatest regret that I have from all my life on earth. Well, maybe not the greatest. My greatest regret was what I told Jill, the day Baby Kate rolled down the stairs.

That was the most horrendous day of my whole life. Kate and Jill were always so cute when they played hide and go seek on the front porch. It was such a beautiful fall day; I wanted them to get some fresh air. I should have just sat with them out there instead of worrying about getting the potatoes mashed for dinner. I could have waited until William got home.

As soon as I turned off the hand mixer, I was greeted by screams, "Kate!"

I jetted out the front door only to find the foldable gate swinging wide open. That stupid gate. The clamp on it always gave us a hard time. William promised he would stop at Caldors and pick up a new one, but he never did. Jill and Sandy were squatting next to Baby Kate, lying on the sidewalk at the bottom of the stairs. Some neighbors, I don't remember exactly who, were starting to filter into our yard. Someone must have called Sandy's mother, because I remember her, flying across the lawn, looking down at Kate and saying to me, "Oh my God, Helen, I will call an ambulance!" Then she disappeared into the house.

"My baby, my baby, Kate, wake up!" I sobbed as I reached down and held her precious, innocent face in my hands. Baby Kate's face was lifeless. Her piglet pink coloring started to ashen. "You were supposed to be watching her, Jill! THIS IS ALL YOUR FAULT!!!" I have never raged before or after like that. These words were my biggest life regret. What made it even worse, is that I never went back to this moment, to these words, to repair the damage they did.

Chapter 31

JILL
DECEMBER 29, 1995

Memories that had been fossilized deep inside of me were being excavated and exposed to the day of light. Tears streamed down my face and I wanted to throw up the meatloaf dinner that I had just consumed.

I remember that day, or thought I had. I remember playing with Kate, when Sandy came peddling up to the porch ringing the bell on a brand new purple bike with glittering tassels flowing from the handlebars. "Look, Jill, look what my grandparents brought me for my birthday!" She said excitedly.

"Wow!" I screamed enviously as I headed for the gate, leaving Kate holding Boo.

Sandy jingled the bell again as she pulled to a stop at the bottom of the stairs. "I hope I get a basket for it at my birthday party on Saturday so we can ride around and pick flowers!" Jingle, Jingle. "Do you want to try it?"

I paused for a second, but just for a second, thinking of Kate. "I'm watching Kate, but I guess I can just ride it on the front sidewalk here." I said as I opened and shut the gate. I remember now, it was hard to line up the clasp to the round hoop it was supposed to grip. I used both hands and thought I got it properly closed, then I headed down the stairs. What would be the harm, we were right there.

Sandy's bike was the most beautiful bike that I had ever seen. The shiny purple paint had a hint of glitter that sparkled when the sun hit it just so. The wheels were crisp, clean white. The only thing marring this perfect vehicle, was the bright orange flag waving above our heads attached to the back wheel. When I looked at it, Sandy, admitted, "Yeah, I know, dorky. My dad made me put it on. He said that way drivers can see me better."

I concurred, and made a mental note that I could not let my dad see this or I would have one on my bike, too. I hopped on the banana seat decorated with multi-color flowers and cruised up and down the sidewalk. "Wow, this is a really nice bike!"

As I took my third loop down the front sidewalk, the event that changed our family forever, happened. I didn't see it. I only heard the sound of Kate's rolling walker thrashing down the stairs, a brief cry from Kate and then silence. When I turned around, Kate was lying sideways in her chair and wasn't moving. I remember Sandy and I running to her as Kate lay still on the sidewalk.

Until reading the diary, I didn't remember anything else. I must have been in shock. I just remember people running all over the place. The next thing I remember was Sandy's mom ushering me to her house. My mother's journal description of the scene tore my heart out. The pain that I must have felt at the time, but sequestered because it was way too much for a six year old to handle, decided it was time to reveal itself. I began to sob, as much as I tried to will myself not to. The pain, the sorrow, the horror stirred all together and the sobs became uncontrollable, too much for the couple sitting in the row across from me to pretend they didn't notice.

The woman leaned over and whispered, "Are you

OK?"

I looked at her and nodded my head, embarrassed at my behavior and overwhelmed by my new revelations. "My mother just died," I choked out. I had to say something and I certainly wasn't going to divulge what was going on inside of me.

The woman looked at me with deep compassion, reached into her pocketbook, and pulled out a small pack of travel tissues. She reached over and handed them to me, "I'm sorry."

My chest expanded, I was relieved when she didn't ask any more questions and went back to sit next to her dozing husband.

I continued to cry, for the loss of Baby Kate, the sister that I had wanted. I cried for my poor mother, all the years that she carried the blame for what I did; for not closing the gate properly. I cried for the way she couldn't bear to go back and try to relieve the blame she added to me. Blame, that I now realized, was the impetus for my need to save people. My great 'aha' moment, all these years I have been trying to undo the fatal mistake I made back on that October day. My life resembled a tragic Shakespearean play.

I remember life was difficult for a long while after baby Kate died. I spent a lot of time at Stacy's house or with my dad. He didn't know how to cook, so we ate at McDonald's a lot. "Your mom isn't feeling well," was all he would say.

Eventually, things got somewhat back to normal. My parents had gone away for a few days and when they returned they sat us down in the living room, Billy and I.

"Kate has gone to live at God's house," my mother said gently to us. "Someday, when we go to live there, we will see her again."

"But, where does she live?" I asked in earnest. "Let's go pick her up."

Mom broke down in tears and Dad hugged her shoulders. "That's not possible, honey. God needs Kate to stay there," He said.

My mother looked like she was in so much pain and sorrow, I didn't dare push the issue. Nor did I ever bring up baby Kate again for fear of hurting her.

With one tissue left to spare, the tears finally stopped flowing and the sobbing turned to deep heavy breaths. A wave of peace washed over me. I felt like I could almost float away. The off button that I had been searching for was finally in the off position.

Chapter 32

HELEN

DECEMBER 29, 1995

As I watched Jill drift off into a deep, deep sleep in her airplane seat, a subtle white light began to glow behind me on the wall. As the light grew in size and brightened, I felt like I was being drawn into it. As tempting as it was, and it was tempting, even more than wanting to sneak a sample of my favorite chocolate chip cookie batter, I felt a stronger pull to stay where I was, at least for the time being. "I'm not quite done here, please, I want to stay just a little longer." The light slowly faded away.

How could I have doubted that my darling daughter, with the oversized heart, would not forgive me. I should have known that my little girl who I used to find sleeping on her bedroom floor as a child, while her stuffed animals slept comfortably tucked in her bed, would not hold my harsh words, against me. I should have told her long ago, but alas, at least was finally aware.. I could only hope that it would free her to go in her own direction.

She was right; life after Kate's death was extremely hard. There were days so dark I thought about ending my life. Alcohol was my only anecdote. It started when Sandy's mother, Angela, came over one night after both of our kids were in bed. She brought a bottle of wine and we sat at my kitchen table.

"How are you holding up?" she looked at me concerned.

"Not well," and I broke down in tears.

She opened the wine and poured me a glass. Normally, I would enjoy a glass now and then at an affair, but never thought to drink more than two and certainly not by myself. That night, however, the wine numbed the burning hole deep inside my chest. Angela left the bottle when she went home and I finished it, rendering myself obliterated and stumbled up to bed.

I felt even worse the next morning. Somehow, I got the kids off to school and William went to the office. I drank a few glasses of water and took an aspirin. That really didn't help. Now I had what felt like a gaping hole in my chest and a headache on top. I meandered around until I found myself at William's bar in the butler's pantry. It was fully stocked with only top shelf liquor. We didn't entertain that often, but when we did, William wanted to make sure he had whatever our guests, mostly clients, enjoyed.

It started with a sip of scotch from the crystal decanter. Soon Jimmy Beam and Johnny Walker were my new best friends. William started to ask if I was OK when he got home. The house gradually filled with dust and clutter. William became suspicious and started confiding with one of his agents, Lori, about what was going on in our home. Lori was just a year or two older than me. Her husband was a chronic alcoholic, with a shiny red veined nose and nine-month pregnant-looking belly. He spent most of his days on the golf course.

What started as a reach for help, turned into commiserating and eventually an affair. William and Lori would meet at empty homes on the market. My checking out, and his guilt for not buying a new gate, left him in unbearable pain too.

If it weren't for Father Peter, I don't know if we would have made it through that dark period. When we began skipping Sunday mass, he started to stop by the house.

"Oh, hello, Helen," he would say when I answered the front door. "I was just in the neighborhood and thought I would stop by and see how you are doing?"

Of course, I'd feel guilty and invite him in, although I was ashamed to. While he put his coat in the closet, I would scurry into the kitchen and hide my glass du jour. "Coffee?

"I'd love some," he'd say as he sat down at the table.

He soon figured out what was plaguing William and me between his impromptu visits and the small town rumor mill. He invited us to his office at the church and of course, we went.

Luckily, our meeting was early in the morning. Although my head was throbbing, my mind was half alert. "William, Helen, I've known you two for a long time. The pain of losing a child before your own life is completed is known to be one of the worst to bear. I'm concerned, however, that if you both don't learn how to adjust to it, you are going to lose more than one child. You will lose enjoying and being part of the life of your two remaining children. I've heard it all too often in the confessional, years later, the regrets. I highly recommend that you two go away to this Catholic couples' retreat." Father Peter held out a pamphlet with sun streaming through clouds over a dewy field on the front.

William took it, looked at it, then handed it to me. Father Peter sat in gentle silence, occasionally slipping his finger into his collar that looked too tight.

I can't say I jumped at the opportunity, but luckily William did. He and Father Peter convinced me to go and I was lucky to be saved before I became pickled in the devil's brew. William and I renewed our marriage vows at the end of the retreat and returned as partners; together we would move forward and pieced of lives back together. He fired Lori and as far as I know he never strayed again until once again, I became weakened.

THE ISLAND

Chapter 33

JILL
DECEMBER 29, 1995

"Ladies and Gentlemen, we are going to begin our descent to Triton Island. The weather is clear and the temperature a pleasant 85 degrees. Flight attendants, please prepare for arrival."

Startled at first as to my whereabouts, I shook off the exhaustion and sat up straight. I used the one last tissue still in my hand to wipe the drool off the side of my mouth. My leg was stiff. I stretched as far as I could in the cramped space where I sat, and tried to unleash the muscles around my injured area that were now webbed with scar tissue.

"Please put your seat in the upright position," the flight attendant said to me as she walked down the aisle. I did as she said, then looked out the window.

Off in the distance, I saw the island we were heading for surrounded with a pallet of blues unlike any I had ever seen before, even in the hardware store paint swatches. I began to question my impulsive decision to come here; I felt the reality that I was alone. Part of me wished my family was here with me; they would have loved being part of this trip. But I only wanted to be with the family I used to have. The burn from the betrayal of the men in my family still smoldered. I decided they didn't deserve to be part of this. Then, I held my two hands, one over the other, atop of my chest and willed my mother to be with me in spirit on this journey. There was no point in turning back, I may as well try and enjoy it. "Do it for the story!" Becky would say.

I stuffed the airline in flight magazine and my mother's journal into my backpack and admired the view that only became more magnificent as we neared the island. Excitement, a feeling I hadn't felt in such a long time, actually snuck in.

The crew landed the plane gently on the runway and the flight attendants reminded the restless crowd to remain in our seats until we arrived at the gate. The sun shrunk to a glowing sliver. As much as I would have liked to head straight to the beach, after I checked in, I felt that maybe a good night's sleep would be best, so I could start fresh in the morning.

Once the plane was securely parked, the flight attendant heaved the plane door open. Moist, sweet air engulfed us like a warm hug. My pores and nasal passages wicked up the moisture quicker than the most absorbent paper towel back home. The scowl that was engraved in my forehead began to melt as it listened to the non verbal communication coming from my fresh tropical surroundings saying, "It's OK, you are safe now, you can relax." Simultaneously my shoulders stopped trying to grab onto my earlobes and one by one the vertebrae in my spine gave each other some space. I felt my face, dry and rough like sandpaper from the raw winter air plump back up, like a raisin transforming back into a grape. It was instantly clear that the makeup I brought would not be necessary. The foundation I was wearing was already starting to feel cakey and would probably soon start running down my face.

One by one, we debarked, climbing down the narrow metal stairway they rolled up to the plane. Together we walked across the tarmac into the one terminal building. After about 15 steps I was able to shake off my minor limp and stride smoothly. Native islanders greeted us, as a group of short, thin, black as tar, men gathered by the planes storage to unload our luggage. I would learn later that these people were actually descendents of African slaves who had been brought here to work the salt industry many years ago.

Entering into the terminal I felt myself saying, We're not in Kansas anymore! A hand painted sign said, "Customs", hung above three simple white desks, each manned by a native islander in a dark blue shirt and shorts. "Welcome to Triton Island! Please line up at each of the three stations and get your customs form and ID out please." The simplicity of their airport was heartwarming, not cold and overwhelming like JFK.

"Welcome little lady, where will you be staying?" grinned an island man who looked to be in his mid 60s. He had many missing teeth.

"Sea and Sand Resort," I said, knowing full well he probably could have guessed that as there were very limited hotel options here.

He stamped my custom form then instructed me to gather my luggage. The men who unloaded the plane were now pulling wooden carts toward a hole in the terminal wall. "Once you have your luggage, go out the door and there will be a shuttle van to take you to the Sea and Sand Resort. Enjoy your stay!"

"Thank you, " I replied, as I stuffed my travel documents in my backpack side pocket and set out to identify my one black luggage bag among all the others.

The couple who sat next to me on the plane was again next to me at the platform. "I'm so excited!" the woman squealed as she squeezed her husband. I focused on finding my luggage before my heart began to yearn for a companion.

Chapter 34

HELEN

DECEMBER 29, 1995

I watched to see that Jill got safely checked in at the resort. She was right; our family would have loved going to this island together! William never wanted to venture too far from home for fear that the business might need something. The only time I got him out of America was for our trip to Greece. He only agreed because he realized that the kids were really moving on with their lives when Billy moved out. I really appreciated Jill's invitation to join her, and I will, but first I thought it best for me to check back on my men.

Responding to the request in my heart, the view from the window I stood at changed. I became a proverbial "fly on the wall" in my own living room. William sat on our couch with his new lady friend sitting next to him, her hand in his. As I mentioned before, I had a very strong suspicion he was having an affair early on after my diagnosis; his lack of warmth and touch, not sleeping in our bed and coming home late. I just didn't have the strength to ask. Actually, I had the strength to ask, I just didn't have the strength to deal with the potential answer. I needed to focus on trying to stay alive, and get rid of the disease engulfing my body.

Luckily, I didn't know this woman. It hurt less than

being betrayed by a woman I knew.

"She's your daughter, she will come around, she'll understand in time," the woman, Marian offered.

William shook his head, "You don't know my daughter, she has very high standards, and I'm not sure forgiveness is in her vocabulary."

I couldn't help but smirk. That's my girl! Now, don't get me wrong, I didn't want my husband to go on feeling shame and suffering. Yet, at the same time, I was comforted that there was some price to pay for breaking our sacred vows. Content that he was in good hands, I moved on to Billy.

I found Billy under the hood of his souped up forest green Chevy Chevelle in his garage. Cars, tools, gadgets, he loved it all, always did. He was always easy to buy for at Christmas, Tonka trucks, Legos, and the annual Hess offering. While knitting and sewing were my personal refuge, Billy's was fixing something.

As I admired my talented son, I blew him a kiss filled with love. As it passed by his cheek, he put his hand there to see what was sweeping by it, then stood up with an inquisitive look on his face. I wanted to say to him, Yes, honey, it's me.

He leaned against the front of the car with the hood standing wide open and just stared at the leaves blowing across the driveway

"Billy, phone for you!" Mindy called out to him from the kitchen window.

"Who is it?" Billy called back, his tone insinuating that he was not in the mood for a phone conversation. He turned around, glanced again at the shiny engine and closed the hood.

"She says her name is Becky, she's a friend of your sister's."

Billy perked up, and with a quickened step, headed for the house.

I made a promise to myself. When I return to heaven, if I ever got to meet God, I must thank him or her or whatever, for providing my men with loving support.

Chapter 35

JILL
DECEMBER 29, 1995

"The Welcoming Party is on the Coral Deck, it begins at 9 pm. Just follow the seashell path to the music," the dreadlocked gentleman instructed me as he handed me a key and whistled for one of the bellboys to help me to my room.

A thin man a half-foot shorter than my 5 foot, 7 inches came forward with a beat up luggage cart. "Just one bag?"

I nodded.

"This way, please."

"Did you grow up here," I asked, trying to make conversation

"Me, oh no, I come from the island to the west three years ago. We have very few jobs there."

My own problems took on a new perspective. "What about your family, did they come here too?"

"My brother did, he work in the kitchen here. Everyone else is back home. We try to send them money when we can."

"So is the grass greener here?"

He just looked at me, head cocked to the side like a puppy dog.

"It's a saying," I added. "It means do you like it here

better?"

He pushed his shoulders back. "Yes, yes, for sure, but I do miss my family back home." The bellboy reached for the key in my hand. With a few jiggles in the lock, the doorknob turned and the white washed door flew open. "Welcome to your home away from home!"

I walked past him as he stood waiting for me to enter first. There was a queen sized bed coated with pure white comforter. A mosquito net hung above it bundled at the top near the ceiling with the flowing ends bundled and tied at each side of the headboard. It reminded me of a bride's tulle train. The Tuscan style tiled floor was still damp from being freshly mopped. The sand colored drapes were pulled back from the windows.

"Shall I leave your bag here?" Darly, his name tag I noticed for the first time, asked.

"Yes, that will be fine, thank you, Darly."

Darly smiled at the sound of his name. I handed him a twenty dollar bill.

His eyes and mouth opened wide and he held the twenty out to me. "Thank you , Miss, but this is way too much."

I wanted him to take it graciously and leave, not make me feel like I was placating him. "I want you to have it, please. I appreciate your help and I'm sure that if I need anything during my stay you will be as helpful then too. And, my name is Jill."

I clearly made an ally here, as Darly stuffed the bill into his pocket, "Thank you, Miss Jill! You need anything during your stay, you just call for Darly!" Off he trotted.

Part of me wanted to just stay secluded in my room. Maybe read a little, take a shower and go to bed. But it seemed wiser to go, at least for a little while, to the party and see what this place offered. So I showered, donned my flowered sundress and flip flops; and headed towards the music I heard in the distance.

The sandy path, lined with the brown and white Triton seashells that I read about in the airplane magazine, was dimly lit with tiki torches. The path meandered through lush, hardy vegetation. As I neared the sound of steel drums and conversation infused with laughter, I stopped for a moment to admire the swaying palm trees above, each with a cluster of coconuts at the base of the fronds.

"Do you like coconut?" a cheery, deep voice asked from behind me.

I turned to find a guy, about my age, with dark skin, but not nearly as dark as the island natives. His shaggy black hair, trailed across his right eye, which he flicked back with a shake of his head. His voice had an accent I couldn't place—like a cross between someone from Michigan and a Native American from Arizona.

"Ummm," I said, caught off guard. I looked up at him, "I think so. I have only tasted coconut that comes already shaven in a bag."

"Oh, you must put trying fresh coconut on your list of things to do while you are here! But for now, come, you don't want to miss the party! Can I buy you a drink?" Suave. Sexy. As he passed by me, his scent smelled of coconut. He was tasty too. He walked in front of me, and waved for me to follow. Once I stood on the deck, however, he disappeared into the crowd.

Although I am not normally a big drinker, a pina colada was definitely needed; even if it only provided me with something to hold and helped me look like I fit in. It didn't look like sexy guy was going to buy me a drink, so I headed for the bar. The crowd was very mixed: couples who looked like they would rather be alone, groups of gals who made this journey together, a couple of groups of guys who were eyeing the groups of gals, and a few dotted singles like me. No families, no kids.

With a pina colada in hand, complete with a triangular slice of pineapple clinging to the top rim, I headed over to the center of the deck where a bronze mermaid fountain flowed. The mermaid reached out with one hand towards the sky with a Triton shell in her hand. Her long hair flowed behind her. It made me wonder if it was possible that mermaids really existed. There was something about this new atmosphere that had possibility in the air.

I sauntered over to the edge of the deck overlooking the beach that led to the sea. The water spit out a foamy froth, the result of being pounded on the sand a million times. The moon was no where to be found tonight, so I could only use my imagination of what lay out beyond where the deck lights lit.

"Did you just get here, too?" Asked a thin guy too thin for my liking, about my height. I just can't see myself with a guy my height or shorter. What if I wanted to wear heals?

Stupid question, I thought, given that this was a welcoming party for new arrivals and we all had the same complexion, pasty white. But, I gave him a friendly, "Yes, just an hour ago."

"Where are you from?" he asked taking a swig of his Corona.

"New York, and you?"

"Chicago, we got out just in time, they were forecasting a bad storm there."

Behind Mr. Chicago, Mr. Dark Handsome Dude chatted with a group of girls. Clearly he enjoyed, and was comfortable, being the center of female attention. I berated myself for feeling jealous of a man whose name I didn't even know his name and who Becky would have labeled a "Dog." You know, the kind of guy you stay away from. A player.

I didn't have to come back with more conversation because a spunky gentleman and woman jumped on the stage and grabbed a microphone shouting, "Welcome to Sea and Sand, Heaven on Earth, everyone! Are you ready to have fun!" The crowd cheered in response.

"Awesome! Dahlia and I are here to outline all the ways you can have a fabulous time while you are here with us!" With that they shot off every activity that you could think of that had to do with the beach and sea. Sailing, snorkeling, scuba lessons, scuba diving, beach volleyball, windsurfing, beach barbecues, tennis, water volleyball and on and on they went offering more than a Greek diner's menu. By the time they were done, I had finished my pina colada and excused myself for the night. I would stick with my plan, get a good night's sleep and think about trying some of the activities tomorrow or just relax and read on the beach. Mr. Chicago looked disappointed by my exiting, Mr. Dark and Handsome didn't even notice.

Chapter 36

HELEN
DECEMBER 30, 1995

The rays of the rising sun danced in the distant horizon turning darkness into shadowy figures. The introduction of what was on this magnificent island was so exciting, I couldn't wait for Jill to wake up.

I watched the island slowly start to rustle. Resort workers cut fresh mangos, bananas, and oranges for the breakfast buffet. Men quietly raked seaweed that had washed up on shore over night off the beach. They were lost in their own thoughts.

The sea was especially calm this morning. It gently unfolded onto the beach, like a page turning in a book. It was still too dark to see if the sky would be clear or cloudy.

I always loved the tranquility of the early morning. That was the time when I would make the kids' lunches for school, bake fresh muffins for breakfast or just enjoy a few moments of alone time with my needle and thread. For once the day brightened, my day often became one big To Do list.

I wished I could spend the whole vacation with Jill. I wished she would meet a nice guy, one that deserved her. I kicked myself for all the times that I told her she should stick with Jack. Whoever said, Mother Knows Best, surely wasn't a mother! Mother Wants Best for her kids would be more apropos. I knew that I would have to return to heaven soon, but there were a few loose ends I just wanted to tie up here.

In the distance, I saw only a single cloud in the sky. It was dark gray, but alone. There was a very good chance that it was going to be a beautiful day!

Chapter 37

JILL

DECEMBER 30, 1995

I know you're there by the rainbows I see,
I know you're there watching over me,
I know you're there by the sound of the crow,
I know you're there,
I know you're there.

Morning light cracked through the drawn curtains and hit my eyes like a laser beam. Annoyed at first, I pulled the covers over my head and buried my face into the pillow. When my consciousness awakened, I threw the covers off, excited to finally see what the resort really looked like.

I pulled back the curtains, slid the glass door open and stepped out onto the small balcony that held two wicker chairs with a small matching table in between. I drew the deepest breath that my lungs could absorb of the sea filled air. As I exhaled, I heard the words that I had just woken up to, repeating in my head:

I know you're there by the rainbows I see,
I know you're there watching over me,
I know you're there by the sound of the crow,
I know you're there,

I know you're there.

"*I know you're there.*" Who knows I'm here? The words played, over and over, in my head like a song. If I could sing, I may have actually tried to perform it. The chorus repeated. It was relentless, as I stood on the balcony and marveled at the view of the ocean, the tropical gardens and crystal white sand. Way off in the horizon, a single gray cloud hovered. The cloud had streams of silver running down from it towards the ocean, rain I presumed. Within a minute, it slowly moved further away and left behind the largest, brightest, ROYGBIV rainbow that I have ever seen! "I know you're there." The verse repeated itself only as long as the rainbow was in view, then my mind went quiet. I smiled, cried a tear of joy, and mouthed to myself, "Thanks, Mom." She sees me. I knew it. I didn't travel alone after all.

There was something so renewing and promising about the island that I didn't want to waste a second of it in my hotel room. I fumbled through my suitcase, pulled out my new yellow bikini, ripped the tags off with my teeth and tied it on. I covered up with shorts and a T-shirt, packed my backpack with reading material, sun block, slid my feet into my flip flops, covered my eyes with my sunglasses and headed to the beach. I felt a dull ache in my leg and shoulder, but I knew with some walking, the pain would even out.

The towel station was not yet open, but a few folded Sun and Sand teal beach towels were folded on the front desk for early risers like me. I grabbed one, and tucked it into my bag.

Out at the beach, I found myself alone. Apparently, the other guests must have stayed at the party last night much later than me. Undaunted, I walked across the baby powder sand until I hit the ocean. I braced myself for the initial shock of cold that I was used to at home, but instead, the water flowed over my toes as smooth and warm as bath water. I ventured in further, and further, and only stopped because I didn't take the time to take my shorts off or put my backpack down. My leg muscles unclenched. I looked down and in amazing detail saw my feet, toes polished hibiscus fuchsia, standing next to a starfish the size of a dinner plate.

As I stood there in awe of this, I heard a giant splash coming from the dive boat moored just 30 feet out from me, the only boat in the bay. I looked up to find the source of the splash, but only gentle ripples remained. I stared at the site, hoping whatever splashed the first time, would cause a splash again. Seconds, which felt like minutes, passed. But then I saw a fin! A stone gray fin, smoothly cut through the calm water. And next to it, something else, it looked like a swimmer! What is someone doing out there with a shark?

Frozen and mesmerized, I watched as both the swimmer and fin disappeared. They resurfaced a few feet away from where they just were. Then again, they disappeared, and re-appeared. Finally, the swimmer popped his head up, and took off his snorkel and mask. The fin resurfaced further out to sea, heading away from the swimmer. Noticing me, the swimmer waved. I squinted, and realized, it was Mr. Dark and Handsome!

He began swimming towards me. I waited, much too curious to know what, who, he was swimming with. He paddled up alongside me, and sat on the ocean floor, his head just above the water. "Good morning!" he beamed.

"Was that a shark?" I exclaimed.

Mr. Dark and Handsome just chuckled, "No, that's

Sharky, he is a bottlenose dolphin. A lot of people think he's a shark. That's how he got his name!"

"But, you were swimming with him," I said, dumbfounded.

"Yes, Sharky, is what we call an ambassador dolphin. He is one of just a few dolphins in the world who swim alone; normally dolphins swim in a pod. He likes to interact with people, but he is totally free, it is of his own free will that he does this. I have been swimming with him since I came to the island. He swims with a lot of the dive team too."

"But, why, why does he swim alone?"

"No one is quite sure, "he continued. "There are theories that he may have been released after being captive or maybe a storm separated him from his pod when he was young?"

"How long has he been doing this?" I asked.

"Well, I have been here three years now and from what I am told he has been swimming with people on the island for at least six years now."

Mr. Dark and Handsome stood up and shook the water from his hair. His sculpted, triangular swimmer's body was luscious and it made me lust inappropriately for him. I hadn't noticed his dark, chocolate brown eyes the other night, but they pierced my very being now.

"Do you always swim with your clothes on and bring your backpack in the water?" he chided me.

I looked at myself and realized that I looked as overwhelmed by the beauty around me as an Iowa farmer visiting Manhattan for the first time. "Um, no, I was just checking to see the temperature of the water. The water that I'm used to is dark and ice cold. You can't see your feet when you walk in."

"And where would that be?" he asked.

"New York, I'm sure you've met a lot of us."

He shook his head, yes.

"You're not from here?" I asked curiously.

"No, I'm from Hawaii. I heard about the great diving here in Triton, so I came here to work as a dive instructor."

I couldn't go on calling him Mr. Dark and Handsome all week. "My name is Jill," I offered as I extended my hand, way too business-like.

"Bane," he countered and shook my hand, while his pupils dilated.

"That's an interesting name," trying to keep the conversation going and holding his hand way longer than I should have.

"It means 'long-awaited child,' I have three older sisters back home. My parents wanted a son. It took me a while to get here," with that I withdrew my hand and he his. Three. We could have been three; a girl, a boy and a girl.

"Well, I have to go and collect my morning dive group. Do you dive?" he asked as I followed him out of the water.

"Me no, I've snorkeled, in a pool. But scuba dive, no, not sure that I am ready for that!"

"Snorkel, in a pool? What fun is that? What do you look at, the black swim lines on the bottom?" his muscled chest glistened with sea water.

I was clearly a proverbial "fish out of water" here. I began to feel uncomfortable, inept.

"Tell you what," he offered. "I don't have a class this afternoon. How about if I take you to Conch Cove and show you some real snorkeling."

The brochures I leafed through at the front desk depicted a completely different universe under the waves here. I pushed away the fear and took him up on his offer, "Sure, that would be great!"

"I will pick you up at the front desk later, at one. Be sure to stop at the sports shack and get yourself a mask, snorkel and fins."

"OK!" I said way too enthusiastically.

He smiled, turned away and walked toward the sports shack.

Chapter 38

HELEN
DECEMBER 30, 1995

Ahh, yes, young love! It was so exciting, those early moments when you meet someone who makes you feel like you are the only two people on the planet and life can do you no harm. William and I were like that once.

I am glad that Jill felt my presence with the rainbow. I hope she will remember that I will always be with her, always love her. The pull from the other side got too strong for me to resist, it was time for me to go home.

Chapter 39

JILL

DECEMBER 30, 1995

Would I look too desperate if I did my hair and put makeup on, I wondered? No, it was probably not a good idea, the last thing I needed was mascara running and fogging up my snorkel mask. Maybe I should have bought a sexier bikini. I could have brought one "just in case." Why was I so closed minded to meeting someone? In the end, I settled on the royal blue bathing suit, cut high at thighs, so it accentuated my legs. After all, I had been frequently told I had good legs. I still do, but now one has a long scar on it. I wrapped myself with the vibrant lemon colored sarong that I picked up from a woman selling them on the beach, under a palm tree, earlier that day.

I parked myself on a teak bench by the front entrance of the resort a half hour early. The time alone allowed me to catch up with myself, and up until then, I hadn't thought of home. Becky would have called my brother and I am sure Billy would have called my dad. I knew that they would worry, and part of me felt guilty about that. I knew I couldn't abandon them forever, but I decided I would deal with that when I got back home.

Darly passed by rolling the luggage cart. "Going somewhere, Miss Jill?"

"Snorkeling," I said as I smoothed my sarong.

Bane pulled up in front of the resort. The clock said it was 1:10. His Jeep had no top on it, and by the look of the rusted areas in the interior, I ventured to guess that perhaps it never did. His smile was genuine as he said, "Hop in!" and it made me smile too.

"Have fun," Darly mumbled as he walked away gently shaking his head.

I tossed my gear in the back seat and climbed in the front seat ready for our adventure. We zipped down the only main road on the island, the same road I had traveled on from the airport. It was pointless to try and have a conversation, we would have had to shout to be heard, as my hair whipped around in the wind and the radio blared some local Triton tunes. Other than an occasional turn of the head to flash me a smile, Bane focused on the road, looking totally at ease.

At the rotary, an exit to the airport was one option, but we looped further around and took the exit that headed south. We drove through the neighborhood where the locals live, a sharp contrast from the resort area. There were one-story shanty homes, with metal roofs and chickens roaming freely around the dusty yards. Small children gathered here and there running after each other while somber looking women hung clothes on lines in their yard.

As quickly as we entered the part of the island where the locals lived, we left it, and drove up and over a steep hill. At the peak was a vista nothing short of spectacular. Bane pulled to the side of the road to let me soak it all in.

"This is Salt Sound," he said.

My initial reaction was to reach into the back seat and grab my camera, but I didn't bother, knowing that a photograph would never capture the magnificence of this moment. Before me lay an alcove of aquamarine colored water. It was nestled among gentle hills on both sides with lush green vegetation. An occasional luxury home dotted the hillside, each clearly designed to capture the view with their layers of verandas and sliding glass doors facing the sound.

"The whole bay is only about two feet deep, until you get to the outlet." Not a soul waded in the water or lay on the beach.

Bane pointed out which celebrities owned which of the homes. "They're hardly ever here, though."

My mind tried to comprehend why someone wouldn't want to spend every living moment here.

After the shock and awe settled in, we continued on. Bane shifted the Jeep down to second gear and made a right turn onto a sandy, unpaved and bumpy road. The bushy shrubs scratched the windshield and attempted to whip my face but I leaned into Bane, secretly happy to have the opportunity to get closer to him. My cheek brushed against his muscular shoulder, making me long for more. In the distance I could see bright white sand surrounded by clear blue sky. Eventually we burst out of the bush, into a private oasis.

"Sorry about the bumpy ride there, " Bane said as he turned the Jeep off. "The best part of this reef is that hardly anyone comes here. It's not all beaten up by tourists."

Unlike the large swaths of beach at other parts of the island, this section was just a small patch of sand with dense beach vegetation surrounding it.

The beach sloped down gently to the water's edge, which was almost as still as a lake. Unlike the very subtle color changes in the bay Sea and Sand was on, this part of the sea had stark contrasting colors as if someone took a canvas and splattered it with multiple shades of blue, green and blotches of black.

"We couldn't have asked for a better day to snorkel. The water is perfectly calm," Bane announced.

I pulled out my beach bag filled with towel, water bottle, sun tan lotion, hat, sunglass case and wallet with my right hand, my collar bone gave a sharp twinge. I grabbed the bag filled with snorkeling gear in my left. Bane simply whipped off his gray cotton t-shirt with Aloha written across the front, tossed it in the back of the Jeep and grabbed a snorkel and mask.

I laid all my paraphernalia on the beach, and traded clothing and sunglasses for swimsuit and snorkel gear. "You're not wearing fins?" I asked.

"Nah, we are just going to hang around the reef. You can, though. You may be more comfortable."

Bane gracefully slid into the sea, as if he were part man, part seal. He paddled out a bit and waited for me. Trying not to look too much like a clod, I strapped everything on in the knee-deep water. I paused for a moment, and pushed the hair away from my face and swallowed. Would my leg and arms hold up? I refused to miss this opportunity. I stretched my arms above my head one last time and headed out to meet him. As I approached Bane, he pulled his mask over his eyes and nose and submerged himself. I followed his lead. He gave me the thumbs up sign as I lay on the water's surface just a couple of feet apart from him and I gave him the thumbs up sign back.

I was instantly over stimulated by the underwater ballet performing around me! Life, previously unknown to me, hustled and bustled all around. I felt like an eagle, souring over a busy city at rush hour. Coral in all shapes and colors lined the ocean floor like mountains. Fish in all colors, brighter and shinier than the fancy sequin dress I wore to my prom, pecked away at algae lining the coral, or swam in formation, like migrating geese. Deep purple fan coral swayed in the underwater current, its base anchored into the coral resembling a brain. I could see over 100 feet around me before a deep blue horizon lured in the deeper water. The inability to speak and share my thoughts made the experience all the more intense. Completely mesmerized by what surrounded me, I failed to notice that Bane had parted from me. Like a child who realizes she is lost from her mother in a crowd, I frantically scanned around me. About 20 feet to my right, I saw Bane's feet gently paddling away into a much darker area.

With a few strong kicks of my flippers I was quickly by his side once again. My right leg began to throb a bit. Below us now, about 12 feet deep, lay a thick bed of sea grass. The water, no longer lit by the reflection of the sun off the sand, was dark and eerie. I felt more vulnerable. Bane paused and just hovered. I looked at him; then surveyed the water around me. He gently scanned the ocean floor. This was beginning to creep me out. What was he looking for? Was there a shark in the area? My heart began to race and I thought about bolting back to the safety of shore. Then Bane gently lifted his right hand and pointed ahead of us. About 10 feet ahead, a sea turtle as large as a manhole cover eased its way off the grass towards the surface. As it floated to the top, like a balloon floating towards the sky, it released a stream of air bubbles. We swam towards it and met it at the surface.

Neither surprised nor impressed by our presence, the turtle gasped the breath it came for, while we bobbed alongside it; then it retreated back to the bottom. Bane gathered a breath as well and ushered the turtle back to its feeding spot. Bane's ability to hold his breath didn't compare to the turtles, but it greatly outdid mine. My only option was to watch from above.

When Bane returned to the surface, he popped his head out of the water and lifted his mask. I welcomed the opportunity to join him back in the world that I normally inhabited to get my bearings.

"That was awesome!" I exclaimed, releasing my excitement.

"The turtles are pretty cool, aren't they?" Bane returned. "Are you doing OK?" He kindly asked.

"Yeah, this is great!"

"Let's head out that way," Bane pointed farther out to sea. I never would have ventured out that far on my own, but with my own personal sea escort, I felt more daring.

As we gently paddled our way along, I saw two more turtles grazing in the grass. Once out of the darkened area, starfish, conch and sand dollars nestled in the sand below. I sensed something haunting behind me. When I turned to check if my instincts were correct, a multitude of slick, silver, beady eyed swords stared at me with razor shape teeth lining the outside of their mouths, just waiting to take a bite out of me! Seemingly completely unaware of what was after us, Bane continued to swim forward. I slowly reached out to grab his arm so as not to launch an attack from our stalkers. Bane looked back at me, I turned and pointed at the army that was getting closer. Bane stopped, pointed upward and popped his head above the water. Reluctantly, I followed, how would I defend myself if I couldn't see my attackers?

Panicked, I cried, "What are we going to do?"

Bane chuckled at my terror, "It's OK, those are barracuda, they won't hurt you, they are just curious."

"Curious, did you see their teeth! And their eyes, they're so intense!"

"Just ignore them and keep swimming, eventually they will get bored and move on." I wasn't done objecting to our company, but Bane resumed his journey and I would be damned if I would let him leave me behind with the hyenas of the sea preparing to eat us alive.

Sure enough, the next time I looked back the barracudas were gone. Whew. We came upon another mountain of coral, some of its peaks actually jutting out of the sea's surface. We swam around it, stopping to gaze into the crevices to see who was home. Eyes of eels and lobsters looked out. Anemones and urchins that I had only previously seen on nature programs clung along the nooks and crannies. Giant multi-colored grouper wove through tunnels. Ironically, the more we just remained still and observed the coral, the more life we saw. Time lost all meaning, the Zen state I was in erased all thoughts from my mind and every muscle in my body relaxed.

Just as I was enjoying this amazing state of nirvana, my adrenal glands released a flood gate of cortisol to react to what was coming. Deep in the blue horizon, a large gray figured loomed and it was heading towards us! I didn't know how much more of this I could take. The roller coaster of highs and lows was getting to be too much. Now I really got myself into a pickle, I thought. Last check we were at least 300 yards from shore, way too far for me to try and out swim the predator just 50 feet away. This time, I didn't need to warn Bane, he already saw it. I tucked behind him, awaiting some type of instructions. When Bane decided to swim towards it, I thought I would choke on the water that I had allowed into my snorkel. Panic started to set in, water was getting into my mask too, and the salt water stung my eyes. This is it, I'm going to drown, rushed into my mind. I had no choice but to surface and let matters in the undersea world take their course.

Gasping for air, I surfaced coughing water out of my lungs. Despite what I had been told, I took the risk of losing my mask and snorkel by ripping them off my head and holding onto them with one hand, while the other hand treaded water to keep me afloat. When my eyes finally adjusted and my lungs were sufficiently filled with oxygen, I calmed down, and started to laugh at myself. On the far edge of the reef the neon green tip of Bane's snorkel trailed alongside a dorsal fin. It was Sharky!

I traded my fears of the unknown for the excitement of what was around me. As fast as I could, I reorganized my gear and set off to join them. When I caught up, I found them playing peek-a-boo around a coral wall. The gentle swishing sounds of the water were now accented by the click and squeaks of the dolphin. When they rose to gather air I joined in right beside them.

"The most important thing to do if you see him," Bane had instructed me earlier in my trip, "is don't try to touch him. He doesn't like that. Just keep your hands to your side, if he wants to touch you, he will come to you." I did as he instructed me so as not to offend Sharky.

I was completely honored to be in Sharky's presence. Is this what it would be like to meet an alien in outer space? Obviously, Sharky knew that we were there or at least that we existed. Bane and Sharky wove through the coral reefs together, like two friends who met at the park to play.

When I had the opportunity to be close to Sharky, I couldn't help but stare into his eye and wonder, what was he thinking of all of this? It was deeply intimate. His body was twice the size of mine, which surprisingly, didn't intimidate me. Bane drifted away behind us, allowing me quality time with Sharky. As the two of us swam together, just a foot apart, looking eye to eye, it happened. The most amazing, never felt before, feeling of euphoria overtook me! The eroding ache that had been sitting in my chest since my mother died was gone. The throb in my right leg disappeared. I felt like I was officially part of this new universe, and I didn't want to go back.

Far away, a whizzing sound entered our world. Sharky must have heard it before us, because he was already heading in its direction before I became aware of it. As he disappeared into the blue unknown, Bane and I resurfaced. A motorboat scooting by had captured our underwater friend's attention and he was off to follow it.

"Oh my God, that was incredible! I feel amazing!" I screamed as I bobbed in the wake of the boat.

"Yeah, I still get that feeling when I swim with him, it's better than sex!" Bane answered. "What do you say we head back in?"

"Sounds like a good idea, I don't think this day can get any better than that!" As we swam back to shore, I pondered about what happened out there. Whatever it was, Bane and I were some of the few people who knew the power of this dolphin, and that he would bond us in a special way forever.

***

I was so glad that Bane offered to take me to a late lunch, early dinner rather than drop me off at my resort. There was so much I wanted to say and ask. This time on the main rotary, we exited to the west and drove along the shore. I tipped my head back and marveled at the cloudless blue sky. Palm trees danced along the road until we pulled off into a sandy parking lot with a painted rowboat turned on its side filled with Queen conch shells. A wooden sign was nailed along the top of it painted in teal and hibiscus pink color that said, "Conch Creations."

"I hope you like conch," Bane announced.

"Never had it, but I like seafood," I replied. The day was turning out to be one never-ending adventure.

We walked down a short trail with flat cement stones lining the way to an open airy courtyard on the sea. A cabana style bar painted white with electric blue trim was on one side, while a battery powered dancing rosta guy wiggled his hips with a drink in his hand to the tunes of 'Don't Worry, Be Happy" on it. Seaside, a separate shack housed a row of three picnic tables on each side and a counter to the kitchen on the end.

"Heeeey, Bane, good to see you," a couple of scruffy guys, resembling sea hands, cheered from the table on the far end.

"You guys catching any fish out there today?" Bane chimed back.

"Oh yeah, man, they biting today!" The guys each sipped their beers and reached for more of their meal.

Bane ushered me to a table and I sat. The wooden window coverings were propped wide open and I watched as two young boys dove into the ocean in front of us. Occasionally they came up with a giant conch shell and threw it into a small boat anchored next to them.

"They catch the conch fresh here. You won't get seafood any fresher. And, you won't find a better mango colada anywhere. " Bane educated me. I leaned forward to listen and nodded my head as he spoke. "Triton Island has the largest mango grove in the Caribbean. You can tour it if you like. It's the other side of the island." I did recall seeing that in the resorts brochure. Deflated, I wondered why Bane didn't offer to take me there himself. Had he decided he had enough of me already? Stop being oversensitive, I told myself; maybe he has seen it a hundred times already. I always say I should go visit the Statue of Liberty, but I never do. It's not really exciting to tour something that is in your own backyard.

"What can I get for you and your friend, Bane?" a large native island woman asked.

"Hey there, Vilda." Bane looked at me, "What would you like to drink?"

"Well, I guess I must try the mango colada if it is the best on the island. I never tried mango until I got here. I love it, mango juice in the morning, mango chutney over grilled grouper, mango salad…"

Bane ordered the same and a platter of mixed conch for two.

The warm breeze brushed against my face. I didn't want the day to end. How was it possible that my life could change so much in such a short matter of time? I fired questions and commentary at Bane about what I saw that morning, and he answered me when he could get a word in. He listened intently, obviously proud that he had impressed me with our morning adventure.

The conch platter was large enough to feed a family of four. Curry conch, fried conch, conch fritters, conch ceviche, coconut conch and French fries in the center. My taste buds were delighted and decided the curry conch was my favorite, although all of the offerings were delicious. And the mango colada? Ultimately refreshing, sweet and creamy.

"I wonder if you get that same awesome feeling if you swim with a dolphin at one of those swim with the dolphins places?" I asked as I refilled my plate.

"They have one of those captive dolphin parks in

Hawaii. I've tried it, but it's nothing like swimming with a dolphin in the wild. Kinda makes sense, I wouldn't want to share any positive energy if I were being held captive and fed old, frozen fish. Look there," Bane pointed out to the water as giant sea rays flew through the waves gobbling up the conch waste the boys had just thrown back in.

"This place is unbelievable! I can't believe the sea life!"

"It is a unique place," Bane reached for some more conch. "I hope it stays this way. The locals and visitors who have been touched by its wonder work hard to preserve it."

"What do you mean, why wouldn't it stay like this?"

Bane lowered his voice a bit, "There are a lot of developers scouting the islands down here. Some airline companies are rumored to be considering investing in expanding the airport and there was even a cruise line looking to create a port here. If that kind of development happens, this place will be like the islands nearby that are overbuilt and commercialized. It will be more like a city lining the beach than a natural habitat."

"Why would they want to do that? This place has so much life in its waters, that kind of development would destroy it!"

"The almighty dollar," Bane's voiced lowered and became monotone. "But we're working to avoid all that."

"How? Who's we?" I leaned in closer, keenly aware that now we were talking about serious matters that didn't need to be heard by the wrong set of ears.

"A bunch of us who care about the environment, " he shared with me. "A major investor already bought 60% of the island and plans on keeping it preserved as it is. When the major cruise company threatened to build a port here, an international campaign put pressure on the island's government and they didn't sign the deal. They are beginning to realize that what they have here is a rare jewel and if they preserve it, it will be worth more in the long run."

The adventurous, exciting, mood of the morning had now turned serious. I wasn't sure I was ready to delve further into the local issues at hand and mar the enlightenment inside of me. At the same time, I was deeply touched and changed by this morning's excursion. The nurse advocate in me wanted to protect and save the lives I now knew existed under the waves. Cruise ships would mean blasting coral reefs, hotel rises would bring huge amounts of waste and runoff, more planes would bring more people to trample the island.

I thought about an interview I saw on TV with Bono from U2. Bono described how during a visit to Africa a very poor man begged Bono to take his son because he could not afford to feed him. The poverty and desperation left Bono forever changed and triggered him to do all the charity work that he does. Would helping this island protect its natural resources be the price I would have to pay for seeing it? After reading my mother's journal, I now knew I had a choice in how I reacted. Perhaps I could be part of the cavalry, rather than trying to be the knight in shining armor.

I looked back out at the sea. The locals lived such a carefree, simple life. Being from New York, I knew the greed mentality of the people Bane talked about. The locals wouldn't even know what hit them until it was too late.

"How about some dessert?" Vilda stood over us and smiled.

Bane looked at me.

"Oh no, not for me, thank you, I'm completely stuffed! I will try and save room for that next time I come," I smiled back, hoping that I would get the chance to return.

***

I thanked Bane profusely when he dropped me off at the resort. The day's escapades had made my vacation completely worthwhile. I didn't want it to end. When he didn't ask me about my evening plans, I bit my lip and asked, "So, what are you doing tonight?"

Bane shrugged, "My mates and I are meeting at the Coconut Bistro. It's a local joint, about a half mile down the beach from here. You are welcome to join us if you like, we'll be there probably around 7ish."

As I hopped out of the Jeep, I turned towards him and responded, "Maybe I will!"

Chapter 40

JILL

DECEMBER 30, 1995 EVENING

I decided to saunter down to Coconut Bistro a little early to catch the sunset. This time I didn't hesitate to really "gussy myself up." I blew dry my hair, and carefully applied my makeup to look as natural as possible. I chose my sexy, strapless, hot pink sundress, that didn't require a bra. I held my open toed heeled sandals in my hand and headed to the Bistro. Not a bone or muscle in my body ached.

The same men that raked the sand this morning were beginning to gather and stack the chaise lounge chairs that dotted the beach. Only a few guests remained, either taking a deep nap or just gazing at the west waiting for the sun to put on its grand finale. Life couldn't be more perfect, as long as I kept my mind focused on the moment I was in.

When I made it around the point, another three mile stretch of beach welcomed me. This new stretch was mostly barren, just long dunes of sea grass and sea grape shrubs with leaves that looked like Mickey Mouse ears. The roof of what looked like a tiki hut jutted out of the dunes about a half-mile down the beach.

It wasn't a long walk to the hut; in fact it was so soothing I wished it had been longer. I took the short faded driftwood path up into the bar area. It was a simple bar, created out of coconut shells, a square deck lined with tiki torches and a few small square tables, each with a halved coconut shells filled with bright pink bougainvillea flowers, placed in the center. I was the only customer.

After dusting the sand from my feet, then sliding my sandals on, I headed for the bar where two happy go lucky bartenders greeted me. One had long dreadlocks, the other a simple traditional haircut. Reggae music played and the two native islanders bounced to the beat.

"Greetings, young lady! Didn't they tell you at Sea and Sand that your drinks are included there?" the bartender with the dread locks cocked his head as he looked at my resort bracelet that gave me away.

"Hi, yes, they did. It's a bit rowdy over there tonight, I was looking for somewhere a little more low key to watch the sunset."

"Ahhh, then you have come to the right place." He handed me a drink menu. "What can I get for you?"

I perused the drink menu, which like the meal buffets back at the resort had too many choices. "What's your specialty?" I asked.

"I make a really good dirty banana!" he replied, his chest puffed out.

"Then that's what I will have."

As the blender whirled, I looked around. A touristy couple sat down at the end of the bar.

"Here you go, one dirty banana!"

"Oh, you going to like that!" the other bartender chimed in, a pudgy man with dark black skin that made the whites of his eyes shine.

"What's in it?" I asked, as I took a sip of the cooling banana flavored drink with a hint of spiked chocolate.

"Banana, kaluha, rum…."

"Lots of rum!" his colleague emphasized.

"Yeah, man!" Damon, at least that is what his name tag said, retorted.

As I sat sipping my drink, I looked out at the sea."I was hoping to see Sharky again." I shared with my new bar friends.

"Oh, you won't see Sharky this evening, no man. Too rough, those waters, right now. He go to the other side of the island when it gets like this." They said in unison.

I sighed and hoped that the ocean would return to calm again soon, as I only had a few more days left on the island.

I could hear a group of people gathering around a patio table behind me. "Hey man, what's happening?!" one of them shouted out to the bartender.

"Not much man, just enjoying another beautiful day in paradise! You boys come out of the ocean for some pleasure?" Damon responded back.

"Yeah, man, that is just what we need," Bane replied as he went up to Damon and his partner giving them each a high five.

"A dirty banana, huh?" Bane noticed. "Better watch out for these guys, they make a mean drink!"

"Don't be giving away our secrets!" both bartenders cried.

I laughed and stood up and headed for the two tables Bane's mates were putting together. As I did, I caught the look Damon gave to Bane, that "You sly dog, always getting the girl" kind of look. Although my gut told me the truth, I needed to stay in my fantasy world for now.

Bane's friends were from all over the world I found out: Australia, California, Israel, and Miami. They all seemed to have grown up as much in the water as on land, surfing, diving, boating. It was no wonder Bane had fish-like skills. They all found out about the opportunity of working at Sun and Sand the same way, word of mouth, from fellow human amphibian types, who traveled around the world.

They shared stories of their undersea adventures with me, one getting more intense than the next. Fighting off encounters with hammerhead and tiger sharks, accidental collisions with fire coral, saving people from Haiti who had capsized out at sea on makeshift boats attempting to find a better world.

"Remember the time when that chick wasn't paying attention to her oxygen and we were 100 feet down the wall?"

"Mate, that was some scary stuff. It was a good thing you were nearby! She could have passed out and sunk into the abyss."

Bane turned to me. "See that line of demarcation out there? Where the turquoise blue turns to dark blue?" he pointed out to sea. "That's where the wall is. The area that is light blue is at most, 40 feet deep. But once you cross the line, to the dark blue area, there is a steep drop that goes down 4000 feet. You can only see down to about 150 feet or so on a bright, sunny day. The wall is lined with coral and it is really cool to swim along it and explore."

"You swim over that line and risk falling into it?" I was deeply intrigued and frightened by the prospect at the same time.

"Do it all the time," one of Bane's mates shrugged as he sipped from his Corona dripping with sweat.

"What is even more cool, is that humpback whales migrate along the wall in the winter. You can watch them travel, hugging along the wall, like a parade, right from here. The whales migrate down to this area from up north to mate and give birth in the early winter. By spring, they head back and you can see them pass by with their calves in tow." Bane shared.

"Tell her about the time you and I rescued the whale," one of Bane's other buddies, Tom, chimed in.

"That was sweet!" Bane tapped the table. "We were out scoping for new potential dive sites to take visitors. We heard across our radio that a boater had spotted a whale in distress. We zipped over to the area, and sure enough, found a whale completely entangled in fishing net from head to tail." Bane paused, took a sip of his beer and continued. "So Tom and I grabbed our snorkel gear, strapped our dive knives to our legs and hopped in the water to assess the situation."

"Weren't you scared?" I had to interject, "Whales are big!"

"Oh, no, not at all. It was a humpback and she was just bobbing in the water, unable to move, desperately sucking in air through her blowhole at every opportunity." Bane replied then continued on with the story. "So we decided to each take an end. Tom started at the tail and I started at the head. I'll never forget the feeling of looking straight, eye to eye, at that whale, just inches away…." Bane paused and looked as if he was drifting back in time. It was, no doubt, one of those magnificent life moments that one never forgets. "We pulled netting out of her mouth, from around her tail and flukes. She didn't fight us at all, she remained calm and still, like she totally understood we were there to help her." Bane paused again, taking another sip.

Tom chimed in, "So it gets better! After she was all untangled, she took a deep breath and sounded."

"Sounding is when the whale dives down into the deep," Bane filled me in.

"We watched her until we could no longer see her, then we climbed back into the boat." Tom continued. "None of us said a word, we were just awestruck by the experience. Then just a few minutes later, the whale came up, right next to the boat, lifted her head out of the water, and looked into the boat, like she was saying 'thanks' and then swam away!"

"And they say that we are the smartest beings on this planet. I really don't think so." The chap from Australia finished off.

"My gosh, that's amazing!" I was impressed and wanted to know more. "But how did she get tangled up in a net?

Yasef from Israel educated me. "Ghost nets are a real problem here. Fishermen leave them behind. Most of them are not discarded on purpose; they get snagged on things in the ocean or break away from the boat due to storms or strong currents. They are made, these days, of such strong synthetic materials they can remain in the ocean for years. The fishing industry is growing rapidly to feed our growing global population so the problem is predicted to get worse."

"That whale was so lucky you guys came to her rescue." I gave them their deserved recognition for a deed well done and they accepted it with pride.

Waitresses began to put candles out on the tables and I realized the temperature had significantly dropped with the disappearance of the sun. As much as I tried not to shiver, the combination of sunburn, sundress and frozen dirty banana was winning out.

"I wish I could stay and listen to more of your stories guys, but I'm afraid I better get back to change." I said.

"Thanks for inviting me to join you, I loved listening to your stories."

"Why don't I walk you back," Bane offered to my surprise.

It did get a lot darker than I realized. "OK, thanks."

Bane's friends carried on amongst themselves, while we settled up with the bartenders and set out to the beach. The more I tried not to shiver, the more I shook. Bane wrapped his arm around me and rubbed his hand along my arm. His warmth made my goose bumps retreat.

We walked in silence. The sky was dotted with more stars than I have ever seen. The potency of the dirty banana made me dreamy. I longed for Bane to turn me towards him, kiss me, lie me down in the sand and make passionate love to me. Once again, however, the walk was too short and we were back at the resort.

"Do you live here, at the resort?" I wondered.

"No, when we aren't working, they don't like us hanging around here, in fact we're not allowed on the property if we aren't working. They have a couple of small apartments down near the marina that some of the staff live. The boys and I, though, share a rental house up in the hills." He pointed way in the distance to the southwest. "It's a pretty cool place, has amazing views."

The tantalizing silence attempted to creep back in, but this time, Bane pushed it away. "How long are you here for?"

"Until Saturday, a couple of more days." I didn't want to think about my trip ending.

We stopped and Bane turned in my direction.

"I would invite you in, but I don't want to get you in trouble."

"It's OK, I need to get back to my mates." He said, but didn't make any attempt to leave.

The urge to unite was growing as the waves lapped at our side and the moonlight now danced in the water. I forgot to breathe and my feet were glued to the sand. Bane gently placed his hand around the back of my neck and pulled me toward him. His lips brushed against mine ever so slightly and my insides tingled. Slowly, he let my face glide away as our eyes engaged. "I'll see you tomorrow."

Chapter 41

JILL

DECEMBER 31, 1995

The residual effects of the rum, from the night before, lingered as I awoke, but nothing so bad that a good cup of coffee wouldn't shake off. The mellow mood of the island was starting to replace my New York go-go-go mentality! It was heavenly to bask in the lusciousness of this island sanctuary. I rolled over and watched the light grow brighter where the curtains didn't quite meet up.

Banes parting words, "I'll see you tomorrow," rang in my mind. The unknown of where and when was unfamiliar to my normally scheduled life. Had I not been tipsy I probably would have asked him, "Where, what time?" The island was only so big, however, just 20 miles long and 15 wide, so connecting with people was almost inevitable.

My mother's journal sat on the bedside table on top of the magazine that I took from the airplane. As intrigued as I was to read what else it had inside, I didn't want to interrupt this feeling of peaceful euphoria that the island was instilling into me. I pushed away all the thoughts from home that were trying to nudge their way in, my brother, my dad, work, the baby, Jack. They were all so far away and not in any way part of this island paradise and there they needed stay for a while. I knew deep inside, eventually, I would need to deal with them.

I lazily rolled onto my back and stared at the ceiling. I sighed and listened to my breathing The ceiling was raised and made of wood strips painted white with support beams running perpendicular to the floor. The ceiling fan, resembling a palm leaf, gingerly spun and blew a gentle breeze that I hadn't noticed feeling before. There was no need for air conditioning. The fan and leaving the window open half way was sufficient to keep the room comfortable at night. I listened for the sound of the ocean but heard nothing. That meant the ocean was calm and I was as excited as a school kid who sees snow,and anticipates a day off from school. A calm ocean meant that Sharky might be in the bay that day.

The clean simplicity of the room didn't trigger any of my problems back home in me. No TV, no radio, just a wicker chair in the corner with a seat cushion covered in red hibiscus flowers and a small dresser that matched. The walls only had two paintings, local artists I guessed; one of a native looking woman weaving a basket, the other of a triton shell alone on the beach.

I toyed with the idea of closing my eyes and drifting back to sleep, but I didn't want to miss all the potential opportunities of the day so I got myself out of bed and opened the curtains. The vibrant sunlight jerked me into the morning and I was glad I didn't return to my pillow.

Rather than go for breakfast right away, I decided to head to the beach. I perused the chaise lounges that had been laid out for the guests, looking for one that would be private, yet close to the water. Activity out on the dive boat caught my attention. I dropped my beach gear on the nearest chair and walked out to the end of the wooden dock.

Bane and his mates were packing up gear. When Bane noticed me, he popped his head up from the boat and yelled, "Hey, there, sleepy head! Are you coming diving with us today?"

With my hand shielding my eyes from the sun, I shook my head, "No, not today!"

He smiled, like he realized what I really meant, which was No, I'm scared to death to dive.

"You don't know what you're missing!"

He was right. Ever since our snorkeling adventure I had to admit I was hooked on the aquatic world. I wanted to know more, wanted to see more, wanted to feel the debate inside me between virgin excitement and sheer unknown terror. But, yes, I was scared, terrified really, to relinquish total control and submerge in the sea.

As I stood watching them ready the boat, a line of black rubber coated divers marched with their gear down the pier. One by one they boarded the boat. Fit, thin, young, along with old, fat and out of shape. The final man, who hung out on the docks edge the longest, in order to finish the last drag of his cigarette, took the cake. Bane caught me looking at him in disbelief, then shot me a reply with his eyes, See, if he can do it, you can. I was running out of excuses.

I simply waved and started back to the beach as Bane helped the last gentlemen on board. "Hey, do you want to go to the Triton Festival later?"

I turned around as Bane awaited my answer while he untied the rope from the boat and tossed it onto the dock.

"Sure!" I shouted back.

The boat pulled away from the dock and I could barely hear Bane shout, "I'll find you later, after lunch!"

I watched as they strolled out to sea and just when I

was starting to lose sight of them, I could swear I saw a fin in the water following them.

***

The Triton Festival was Triton Island's version of what we call a County Fair at home. They celebrated it on New Year's Eve. People representing all the different cultures of the island came out to celebrate all things Triton. The infamous Merman, a sculpted, muscular man at least 6 feet 3, with long dreadlocks woven with shells sauntered around the festival. He wore a glittering green tail. Island kids chased and followed after him laying shells at his feet that they had collected from the beach as tokens to the Merman, Triton.

The island's artists displayed their paintings, woodcarvings, shell jewelry and hand woven baskets and hats. A band played on a makeshift stage, their steel drums luring us in to watch the origin of the sounds. Before we knew it, Bane and I were swaying with the crowd as the lead singer who looked like he needed a good meal crooned, "Ah, yes, ah, yes, we're all part of the Triton Tribe…Ok, Triton Tribe, we are going to take a short break, then we be back and you better have your lungs ready for the Triton Shell Blowing Contest!"

"Are you hungry?" Bane turned to me and asked.

"A little," I replied. I skipped lunch at the resort knowing that festivals usually involve food.

"Let's go see what they are serving," he took my hand and led me over to where rows of tables were lined up. Behind each one stood a proud chef and their team of cooks.

We started at one end and ate our way around the maze of delicacies. Caribbean Spiny Lobster tails stuffed with conch, filleted grouper, fried plantains, tropical fruit sculpted into fish, mango chutney, coconut soup and all things conch; conch fritters, conch ceviche, conch chowder, conch crepes, and curry conch. Triton beer seemed to be the beverage of choice to wash it all down along with mango rum punch.

"Punch or brew?" Bane asked.

"Punch please," I juggled my plates around so I could hold a glass.

As Bane chatted with the bartender, I heard a curt, stern voice behind me.

"Girl, you gonna be the death of me! I toll you to go and get me that extra rag to wipe my hand offs with!"

I watched as a young, maybe 12-year-old girl, walked off with her shoulders clenched to her neck to retrieve a towel from a woven bag behind their food table. A jumbo-sized woman with sweat beading down her temples and forehead shook her head at the girl. When she turned her head, she caught me staring at her.

"And what you lookin' at!" she carried her rant on, now aiming at me.

Stunned, I just stood there. The young girl came back with the towel and tapped the woman's arm, which indented like a balloon being poked at. That's when I noticed the girl's abdomen. The young girl, who stood about a foot shorter than me and was at least two sizes smaller than me, was obviously with child and due very soon. My eyes focused on her belly although I willed them to not look.

"I say what you lookin' at?" The woman shouted at me again, this time louder.

"Hey, Nettie, how ya doing?" Bane carved right through the tension with his smile and charm.

"You tell your today girl not to stare at my

grandbaby!" Nettie wasn't going to simmer down just yet. "You girls from other places think you know it all and can judge me. Well, let me tell you something, you don't know nothing!" Nettie slammed the lid on the pot of whatever she was brewing and wiped her face with the towel the girl just gave her.

"Jill doesn't mean you no harm, Nettie. She's just never scene such a big pot of Conch jambalaya!" Bane's charm was finally taming the bull in Nettie. "Can we have a taste?"

Nettie heaved opened her stewpot and dipped her long wood carved spoon in to fetch us each a cup of her jambalaya. She handed us each a serving and although her tongue was still, her eyes were smoldering. We each blew it several times in an attempt to cool it down, but like Nettie, it was determined to stay hot and pissed off. We each forced a spoonful down, burning our tongues in an attempt to create peace.

"It's delicious!" we both chimed at the same time.

Nettie wiped her brow again and waved us away. "You move on now, I have more people to serve. I need to win first prize this year!"

Glad for the exit opportunity, we each wished her good luck and scoot away as fast as we could. I waited until we were out of sight and earshot before I said to Bane, who didn't seem fazed at all by our encounter, "Yikes, what is up with her?"

"Oh, Nettie," he waved his hand. "Don't mind her, she's just one angry lady. She's actually a big sweetheart, though, when you get to know her."

"But, did you see that girl next to her, who's pregnant at her age?" I asked, still in shock.

"Yeah, that's Trina, Nettie's granddaughter. Trina's mother died at childbirth and Nettie had to take Trina in, probably just one of the things she is angry about." Bane sipped the beer in his hand, then continued. "See down here, men hunt little girls, like sport. It's not like the States. They actually brag amongst themselves when their 'seed is planted.'"

"You mean they get away with rape!" I said, obviously a little too loud as nearby heads turned to look at me.

Bane took another sip of his beer and waited for them to turn away. "It's a different culture." He shrugged his shoulders. "Hey, they're starting the Triton Shell Blowing contest, come on! You should try it!"

Bane pulled my hand and I half rebutted like a stubborn dog that doesn't want to walk on a leash. I wasn't so sure that Bane's acceptance of the local ways was OK with me. Not to mention Nettie's comment about me being his 'today girl,' which was still stinging my ego, which up until now, had been floating up on cloud 9.

He tugged me again and I followed. Once again, the island rum was washing away my normal senses.

"OK, I know my island friends know how we play this game. But for you new comers, here is how it goes!" the whimsical man on stage held up a giant Triton shell with the tip just barely cut off where the spiral ends. "Each contestant picks a Triton Shell from the pile. You line up and each get a turn to blow into your shell and make a sound like this." He took the shell, held it between his two hands, held it to his mouth and blew on it like a trombone. A loud, deep, horn sound came out like we were in the depths of the Swiss Alps. After a very long minute, he let his hands fall to his belly with shell in hand. He took a deep breath, and then continued telling us, "It's not just how loud a sound you can make, it's also how long you can blow it. Our band members will be counting the time." He looked back at them and they nodded their heads, but none had a stopwatch or a pad to write down the results.

"Are you ready? Go pick out your shell!" he pointed at the pile and lifted his own shell to his mouth again and blew.

"Come on!" Bane waved me to follow him. We gathered with the crowd around the shell pile and each picked one. Mine turned out to be larger than his.

"Bigger is not always better," he smirked, "it's how you use it."

"We'll see about that," I slurred back to him as we headed for the line up to the stage.

We patiently waited our turn while our fellow contestants gave their best blow. The results varied greatly from a short grunt, to a soundless spitting, to what sounded like a prolonged ache from a male moose that hadn't gotten any action for a very long time.

"Ah, everyone it is our local dive boy Bane up here next, he can blow!" the host and Bane chuckled with each other and slapped each other five. "Are you ready, man?"

Bane shook his head yes, planted his feet on the stage, took a deep breath, and then let it out into the air. Then he raised his shell towards his mouth, took a second deeper breath, and put the shell to his lips. If the other side of the island didn't hear him, they must have been deaf. The crowd began to silence as the bellowing sound went on, and on, and on. The band members sitting behind him stopped counting at 60 and the crowd began to cheer until Bane finally had nothing left to belt out. He dropped his arms, gasped for a breath and bowed to his fans.

"Yeah, my man, Bane, that is one tough act to beat!"

For a second, I thought about turning around and

running to the bathroom. I knew when I was beat. But the crowd had me pinned on top of the first stair to the stage. There was no way out.

"Ok, beautiful lady, let's see if you can beat that!" our announcer held out his hand and helped me on to the stage. "And what is your name?"

"Jill," I replied shyly.

"Ah, Jill, well you have beautiful lungs. I am sure you can make some noise for us," he smiled and looked at my chest.

For a second I felt invaded, and had we been in the States I might have said something, maybe even kicked him. But here, I was out of my element and I thought it best to just go with it.

"Are you ready?" he looked at me. Bane watched from the exit ramp.

I shook my head, yes, and did as Bane did. Steadied my feet, took a clearing breath, then drew the shell towards my mouth, inhaled deeply and put the shell to my lips. With all my might I blew and all that came out was something that sounded like a big wet fart and the crowd laughed.

The announcer laughed with them and patted me on the back. "Ahhh, little lady, nice try!"

I couldn't help but laugh too as my face felt flush from embarrassment, lack of oxygen or the rum. I wasn't sure.

Bane stood at the bottom of the stage stairs with his hands tucked in his armpits, thumbs visible and pointing up. "See, I told you, it's how you use it!" He added a wink.

We meandered around the festival, Bane stopping to chat with friends, while I tried on jewelry and watched as women had their hair woven in braids with tiny beads like

Bo Derek's. The crowd was cheery and jovial. It almost seemed like a perfect paradise here. They had weather that seemed near perfect every day, no burglaries for there was limited extravagance to long for, and meals were fresh from the ocean or the local fruit trees. I say almost because when we passed by Nettie's table again, to get another drink, her granddaughter followed me with her eyes, looking at me it seemed for help. The dark side that I was now aware of on the island shattered my illusion of a perfect place.

Chapter 42

JILL
NEW YEARS EVE 1995

A late afternoon catnap refreshed me and allowed my liver to siphon out the rum punch from the Triton Festival. Our date ended on such a romantic note. Bane and I exchanged passionate kisses in the Jeep when he dropped me off.

He looked into my eyes and asked, "Have you ever spent the night on a beach on a deserted island?" Then gently kissed his way around my neck.

"No, can't say that I have," I tilted my head back to allow him to explore more territory.

"Oooo, then I have a surprise for you. I will pick you up after my night dive class. Wear something warm." He whispered into my ear.

If the resort van hadn't honked at us, we may have lingered there for hours. Who knows what might have happened. But, I tore myself away from him and promised to meet him on the pier around 10, after the night dive was over.

Something warm. I dug through my wardrobe. The warmest thing I brought was a gray pair of sweatpants with matching sweatshirt. In my haste to get to the airport, I didn't think I would need something warm to wear. I would have to make up for my lack of fashion by wearing the lace thong and matching push up bra that I picked up. The thought of Bane finding them under my workout wear made me all goose bumpy.

I looked at the clock, 9:15. If I hurried, I could get down to the dining room in time to grab a snack before they closed. I wasn't sure what else to bring, so I just stuffed a towel and a hairbrush in my bag.

The resort dining room was beginning to thin out. They were having the big Fire and Dance show, then fireworks at midnight, to celebrate the New Year.

"Just yourself?" the host asked.

"Yes, thank you. I won't be staying long, I want to grab a quick snack."

The host led me to a table that had a clean setting left where two couples were finishing up their dinner. In an effort to cultivate a community among the guests at the resort, long tables lined the dining room, so each could seat up to 10 guests.

The pair of couples looked at me as I sat down, waved hello then continued their conversation in French. I said "Hello" in English and headed for the buffet. I was hungrier than I thought. I piled my plate full of homemade bread, mango, grouper, and fresh seaweed salad. I was glad to see the French pair was surveying their dessert options at the dessert buffet by the time I sat down. I hoped they wouldn't notice how quickly I ate and ran.

With my stomach pleasantly full, I was ready for my evening adventure. Where exactly would Bane take me? How would we get there? I couldn't wait to tell Becky about all this.

As I wandered down the pier, holding my flip flops in one hand and my bag in the other, the sound of dancing music erupted and the glow of flames lit the sky behind me. It's so magical here, I thought to myself. The sky above was more than filled with glittering stars. It was almost completely covered with them and the coal black universe just provided a backdrop for them. I had never seen so many stars in my life. It made me feel so small and part of something so big, so universal..

I heard the sound of the boat and voices before I actually saw it. The night dive only had half dozen or so divers. No way in hell, I thought to myself would I EVER go night diving! The thought of being submerged, in the dark, in a world with millions of alien-like beings all around, held absolutely no appeal to me!

"But it's the best time to see sharks and other creatures that only come out at night," Bane countered to my resistance when we talked about it earlier.

"Sharks, do you really think I want to go in the water with the intention of seeing sharks?" I rebuffed. "Didn't you see *Jaws*?"

Bane only laughed. Our lives were so different, where we came from and what we had been exposed to. It was such a refreshing change to be with someone with no link to my past.

As I stood aglow, waiting for my Prince Charming to finish tying up the boat, I imagined him surrounding me with his muscular arms and kissing me once again. I actually shuddered when he jumped off the boat, and shouted, "Are you ready for your adventure?"

"Yes," I said unconvincingly, now aware that I was going somewhere totally unfamiliar in the complete dark.

"Come along this way," Bane grabbed my hand and the warmth of his hand and its strength put me at ease. I followed him down the pier as his friend, Tom, drove the small rescue boat to meet us at the beach. "Hop on in, your chariot awaits!"

Tom held his hand out and helped me into the boat, while Bane gave the boat a shove out to sea and at the last second hopped in. We were off! To where, I had no idea, but we were headed out to sea.

"Where are we going?" I shouted against the wind.

"You'll see," Bane shouted back.

Realizing that I was just going to have to wait, I sat next to Bane and surrendered as the island music faded away and the glow of the fire dimmed.

It seamed like the ride was about 20 minutes, but we were certainly far enough away from Triton that we could no longer see it. If it weren't for the moon, nearly full and lighting the way, I don't know how they would have found the mound of sand in the middle of the ocean. Tom pulled up to it, and Bane jumped out when it was just knee deep to pull the boat's bow up onto the beach.

Tom handed my bag and a backpack to Bane who threw them up onto the beach, then motioned for me to go to the front where Bane waited to help me off. I followed the command. Bane lifted me in his arms and carried me ashore. I stood surveying my surroundings as Tom pushed the boat back out to sea and reboarded.

Bane waved, "Thanks, Mate! We'll see you tomorrow!"

The island was as simple as a cartoon one that you see in the comics. It was basically just a giant mound of sand where you can see all the edges from where you stood with three palms trees in the middle. I marveled that there existed such a quiet place on this earth.

"So, what do you think?" Banes white teeth shined in his silhouette against the evening twilight.

"This is amazing, but are you sure the tide won't come in and wash us away?"

Bane laughed his laugh at me once again. I was

grateful that he took my fear in stride. Jack would have been very annoyed by now, telling me that I didn't trust him.

I felt like Jane, on that secluded island, with the ocean's version of Tarzan. Bane laid a checkered blanket on the sand and suggested that I sit and relax, which I did. In front of the blanket, he dug a shallow pocket in the sand with his hands then reached into his duffel bag for some old newspaper. He crinkled the paper into balls and tossed them into the pit, then proceeded to gather bits of driftwood from around our private oasis. When he reached in his pocket and pulled out matches I had no choice but to rib him, "What? You're not going to rub two sticks together?"

"I could but it might take a while, " he countered.

The paper immediately took to the flame and created a mass of light and warmth. The driftwood started to crackle until it absorbed the fire and the paper was nothing but smoldering embers. Once again, Bane reached in his duffle bag. This time he pulled out a second blanket, which he laid across my legs. Then he reached in a third time and pulled out two champagne glasses that clanked against each other and a bottle of champagne, dripping with sweat.

"Shall we celebrate the New Year?" he asked as he sat next to me and handed me one of the glasses.

"Sounds like a plan."

As Bane tore away the metal wrapping the cork, he asked, "So, do you have any New Year's resolutions?"

I looked into the fire. I hadn't really put too much thought into it this year. Being down here I lost all track of time. With no snow, Dick Clark and Times Square around, there were no cues to remind me to come up with some ideas. Still gazing into the fire, with the sound of the cork leaving the bottle beside me, I answered, "I have to think about that more. What I do know is that I am going to leave some things behind."

I turned to Bane as he held the bottle ready to pour. I reached my glass out to him. "Like what?"

"I'm letting go of a burden that I have been carrying for a long time; trying to save people." I felt lighter just saying it out loud.

"That's a heavy load to carry, so it sounds like a good thing to leave in the recycle pile," Bane lifted his glass. "To a lighter load in 1996!"

We clanked our glasses and each took a sip of the chilled, fizzy champagne. "What about you?"

"I generally stay with the same motto I have everyday, let me be in synch with what the universe has planned for me."

"I like that. Let's hope that means all good things!" I added.

"To all good things for 1996!" Bane raised his glass and we toasted again.

I gazed back in the fire and watched the streams of smoke slither into the sky like a basket of snakes. I followed it as far as I could see in wonderment. Just how big is this universe?

"You know, I can't thank you enough for all that you have introduced me to down here. I never would have had these kinds of experiences if I had just hung out at the resort."

"It's my pleasure, really. It's fun to have someone to share all this beauty with, especially someone new, kind of like seeing things through a child's eyes."

I looked over at Bane who was holding his glass in one hand and leaning back on his other in the sand. He turned towards me and sat upright. He leaned closer to me and I met him halfway. Our lips gently touched, parted, touched, parted, and then locked. Our champagne glasses fell to the sand and our arms wrapped around each other.

I'm not sure exactly when midnight struck, but I'm pretty sure I left a year of pain behind and ushered in the New Year in ecstasy.

Chapter 43

JILL
NEW YEARS DAY, 1996

I awoke first. Without moving a muscle I slowly opened and closed my eyes to allow moisture to coat them. Straight ahead of me, directly east, the sun too was stretching. At first the horizon was just a hint of yellow-orange, then it evolved into a colorful fruit salad, melon, passion fruit, watermelon, banana. I followed the sky as far as my peripheral vision would allow me, until I could feel the strain on my ocular muscles. The sky morphed into azure blue then became gradually deeper and darker the more I looked west, just like the sea around this island. The lure of what lay beyond my side-glance enticed me. I gave in and allowed my neck to turn to see. Behind me, the still black night still slept.

Bane stirred, pulled the blanket tighter over his shoulders and nuzzled in closer to me. Our naked bodies gave off the only heat on this dewy, crisp, cool morning. I noticed the waves were lapping rapidly this morning, and closer to where we lay. My fear of being overtaken by water calmed knowing that Bane knew the sea as intimately as my mother knew her garden, or a farmer knows his farm.

Both Bane and my mother spent so much time with their perspective natural environment that they knew what its norms were, when it showed signs of storms ahead, when was the best time to do certain things. The inevitable surprises in nature kept them humble. I longed to get more acquainted with nature myself.

It was 1996. A new year, time for a new start. I realized I escaped to this island like a dog retreats alone when it is wounded. But, I had to decide do I lie down and die, or go back into the world. The pilot light inside me said the latter is what I needed to do. The clouds floated by above, reminding me the world was going to keep moving along; it wasn't going to stop just for me.

The watercolor painting above us transformed ever so subtly until it was filled with blue pastel shades. Bane stirred again, this time wrapping his arm around me and kissing the side of my cheek. I lay and soaked up what I knew would only be a short few more minutes of snuggle time before the sun would threaten to scorch us.

Bane kissed my neck and rolled closer. His soldier was rock hard and at full attention. His arm that was wrapped around me lifted and his fingers wandered around my shoulder, to the outside of my underarm and as I became increasingly titillated they teasingly made their way to my breast. We didn't speak a word of English, just the language of pure lust until we lay full of sweat, on top of the one blanket, the other thrown off to the side.

"What do you say we take a dip and cool off?" Bane suggested as he sat up.

"Sure," I sat up too.

Together, we waded into the warm choppy water. Bane went ahead, diving in headfirst. I, on the other hand, entered slowly, until the water covered my chest then dunked my head fully under. Bane swam up to me with a giant starfish in his hand. He flipped it upside down for me to see its many tentacles mulling around looking for something to grab on to.

"I don't think I'll ever get over just how much is hiding under here, " I pointed at the water.

"That's part of what makes it so exciting to dive. You never know what you'll find. They say that 71% of the world is covered with water and we have only explored 5% of it." Bane looked out to the deep. "One time I was out here and I woke up to the sound of a whale spouting. I looked out and there was a mother, right there, resting with her calf."

I raised my eyebrows, because I knew he wanted me to, but a jolt of jealousy hit my gut. He'd been out here before. Of course he had, I reasoned with myself, how did he know we would make it through the night without being blanketed with water? Did he stay out here alone, with his buddies, or with another "today girl"? I couldn't bear hearing it was possibly the latter so I didn't ask.

"We better get dried off and dressed," Bane looked at the position of the sun. Tom will probably be coming soon to pick us up.

Chapter 44

JILL

NEW YEARS DAY-LATE AFTERNOON, 1996

"What do you mean he's missing?" I shouted at Tom.

When the dive boat didn't pull in at four o'clock as usual, I didn't think much about it at first. Life down here operates on a more casual timetable. As 4:30 turned into 4:45, however, I started wondering where they may be. Other resort guests began strolling down the pier, too, looking for their friends and loved ones to return.

"I don't know," I shared with one woman whose husband was out on the afternoon dive. "They are usually pretty prompt."

Her worried look made me worried. Together we went to the dive shack to see what was going on.

"There's been a snag," the unshaven guy at the desk told us as he combed his fingers through his hair. "The boat is on its way in." He turned around and went back to hosing off wet suits that had been used earlier in the day.

"What do you mean a snag?" the wife and I asked in unison.

The guy just continued with what he was doing and repeated without looking at us, "The boat is on its way in."

By the time the boat came in, there were at least a

dozen of us waiting. As soon as I could clearly see the faces of the divers on board, I knew it was more than a snag that had made them late. A snag is when you get a hangnail caught on a sweater or the boat anchor rope gets twisted in a head of coral. No, this was more than a snag.

The buoys along the pier crunched as the boat bounced into them. The guests disembarked one by one, like a funeral procession. Tom was the only dive master on the boat. I stood and bit on my nails waiting until the last diver marched down the pier, "Tom, what is going on?"

"Bane is missing."

"What do you mean missing?"

"He didn't come up from the dive."

I didn't let Tom finish before I was firing questions at him one after another: "But, where is he? Didn't anyone go in and look for him? How could he just disappear?" My voice quivered.

Tom looked to be in a state of shock himself. "Bane was the last guy on the dive line, he was making sure all the guests came up. When we did our final name call, before coming in, we realized he wasn't on board. Yosef went back in but he couldn't find him. Then all of the crew geared up and went in to search. We used up every bit of oxygen in the tanks, but nothing, no sign of him."

I stood stunned, like someone just hit me with a tranquilizer dart.

"We radioed for help and some other boats came out to help. They're still out there looking. I had to get the guests back in. I'm going to load more tanks and head back out."

"I want to come with you."

"Honestly, Jill, it would be better if you waited here. There will be a lot going on in the boats and we don't need a novice that we have to keep an eye on."

As much as I wanted to object, I understood what Tom was saying. It was the same type of answer we gave family members who wanted to stay in the room when their loved one was in crisis in the hospital. "We need you to wait in the waiting area. We are doing everything we can."

Two guys from the shack came stumbling down the pier; their hands filled with wet suits and oxygen tanks.

"We're going to need more tanks," Tom shouted at them. "We only have a few hours until dark."

I got out of the way as the guys scurried faster, loaded the gear onto the boat, then ran back for more tanks. Tom focused on putting everything in its proper place and securing the tanks.

I looked out at the massive fish bowl before me. Bane, where are you?

Maybe he hit his head on the bottom of the boat. But then wouldn't he be lying on the ocean floor, right underneath it? Could a shark have attacked him? If that happened there would have been blood everywhere. My brain began to ache because I couldn't come up with a rational answer no matter how much I strained to do so.

With the boat loaded up, Tom started the engine, his parting words, "We'll find him."

Oh, my God, I hoped so. I felt I was bringing my bad luck to the island.

Chapter 45

JILL

JANUARY 2, MIDNIGHT, 1996

"I see a light, out there, flashing!" I pointed into the darkness.

"Where?" Tom asked urgently as he ran behind me out to the beach.

At first I thought I must have been imagining the light. I had been sitting there in the dark, in a lounge chair on the beach for hours, just staring out at the sea. Sand flies were nipping at my ankles, but the annoying itch was not enough to distract me from my vigil. Tom and his crew had just returned from searching where Bane had gone missing.

Tom and I stood at the water's edge, squinting even though there wasn't an ounce of sunlight to blind us in the dark night. Seconds, which felt like hours, passed before it flashed again, way out, to the northwest tip of the bay. Blink, blink, blink. Stop. Blink, blink, blink. Then it stopped for a long pause.

"There!" I pointed like an enthusiastic terrier that found a duck.

"I see it!" Tom said. "That could be him! Divers in distress use strobe lights to call for help."

Tom sprinted back to the shack. Barefoot, I fought the sand and followed him. "There is a strobe light signaling way out in the bay! Let's take the rescue boat out, it could be Bane!"

One of the guys grabbed a set of keys from behind the counter and hopped over it. Tom ran after him towards the rescue boat tied to a moor just off shore.

"I'm coming with you!" I screamed as I followed right behind them. Sand kicked up from their heels and flew into my face. They weren't leaving me behind this time. If it was Bane, he may need medical help.

The three of us thrashed into the water and heaved onto the boat. Tom undid the rope as the new guy revved up the engine. I looked out for the light. Blink, blink, blink. "There it is!" I held my arm up and pointed directly to the light.

The boat bow pitched up and we were off. Tom and the boat driver stood in the front, while I clung to the seat in the back, the motor whizzing in my ear. My hair whipped in all directions and repeatedly flicked into my eyes.

We screamed across the water, like a scene from *Miami Vice*, short of the white jacket. As we got into deeper water the waves became taller and the boat pounded against them. Blink, Blink, Blink…we were getting closer. I imagined Bane, bobbing in the waves, saying, Hey! Where have you guys been? A big smile on his face. We would get him onboard and he would turn to me and say, I think I need some mouth-to-mouth resuscitation.

The driver cut the engine to a mild gurgle when we got within a few yards of the light, which we hadn't seen blink for a few minutes. We bobbed in the water like a cork. The waves lapped at the side of the boat. The night was partly cloudy, only a few stars dotted the sky. The three of us stood in silence, scanning the water. The moon timidly peeked out from a cloud that it was hiding behind shedding a hint of light. That's when we began to hear the creaking sound, wood creaking like an old rocking chair going back and forth. As the moon shed more light, we saw the tall mast that stood from the large wooden ship just a few feet away.

"Holy shit!" Tom exclaimed, "Let's get the hell out of here!"

The driver was already way ahead of him. The engine roared, our boat whipped around 180 degrees and I was thrown to the floor and didn't bother trying to fight against the force holding me down. We flew across the water, pounding more aggressively against the tide. The adrenaline flowing through my veins didn't allow fear to overcome me, as it should. What was that, I wondered. Why was a big eerie ship that looked like it came straight out of a pirate movie, just sitting there in the dark?

When the boat finally slowed down enough for me to crawl into a seat, I shouted to the guys, "What was that?"

Tom turned around, his hair in disarray, "That was a drug boat. That light you saw was them signaling to someone on shore for a pick up."

My heart sunk. It wasn't Bane and God knows what could have happened to us out there. What was going to happen next on this crazy island?

Chapter 46

JILL
JANUARY 2, 1996 MORNING

"I just don't get it, how could he just disappear?" I heard one of the divers mottle to himself; my sentiments exactly. It went without anyone saying, that none of us wanted to consider the idea that Bane may have sank into the deep abyss. They didn't have deep-sea diving equipment here on the island. Even if they could find someone to bring one of those search subs here, it would take days. Since none of the most apparent explanations were making any sense, conspiracy theories began to creep in. "Maybe someone from one of the development companies, or a local government official on the take, had him kidnapped."

Tom looked at me, his eyes heavy. Neither of us had eaten since lunch yesterday. "We should go and get a bite to eat before the sun comes up."

As much as I didn't want to leave the command center, I knew he needed to eat before he went out to search again. My stomach was all for the idea. We walked to a nearby local eatery.

Tom broke the silence. "I think you should know, Bane talked about you." He said kindly, and then paused. I looked at him. "It's hard for us here. Occasionally, we meet a gal that we really would like to get to know better.

We're cautious, however, because we've all had a time where we fell hard, only to have it not work out when she returns to her real life. This is our real life, but it's not for everyone."

A tear streamed down my face; I didn't know if this made me felt better or worse. Soon I was a complete waterfall, all of the bottled up emotions just pouring out. Tom put his hand on my shoulder. His touch was filled with compassion.

"My flight leaves tomorrow afternoon," I said as I wondered, how in the world could I leave if Bane wasn't found?

"Let's think positive, that we'll find him soon," Tom said.

***

"They found him!" the unshaven, scruffy guy exploded when we returned.

"Where?" Tom and I chimed together.

"They say it will take a couple of hours to bring him back, they are going to take him to the hospital. I guess he's pretty dehydrated."

"What happened, did they say? How did he get lost from the dive boat?" Tom asked.

"The fisherman who radioed in to us said that a tiger shark started stalking him while he was waiting for the guest divers to get on the boat. He swam away to draw the shark. By the time he surfaced, he was way off course, he couldn't even see the boat and he was out of air. He dumped his equipment and the emergency flares slipped out of his hands. The fisherman said he found him way off the north side of the island clinging to an old buoy."

"Thank God that fisherman came along" I said.

"What hospital will they take him to?"

"There's only one on the island. I'll give you a call when I hear that he is back. In the meanwhile you should go back to the resort and get some rest."

***

Tom called as promised and woke me from my nap. He was at the hospital and said that Bane looked great considering his escapade. "I have to go back to the house and get him some fresh clothes. Do you mind grabbing a cab if you come over?"

"Sure, no problem," I said as I jumped out of bed. I didn't bother to shower, just threw my flip flops on and headed for the front desk. I ran into Darly first on the stairs. "Darly, can you get me a cab that will take me to the hospital?" I asked while catching my breath.

"Yes, of course, Miss Jill, you OK?" he put the broom he was using against the wall and gently grasped my arm.

"Yes, yes, I'm fine. They found Bane, he is at the hospital." Word had spread throughout the resort about his disappearance.

Darly let go of my arm, looked down and turned away, "Yes, Miss Jill. I will go and call you a cab right away. It should be here in five or ten minutes."

***

The hospital was small, one level, made of cinder blocks. There was just one main entrance. Immediately inside there was a small room with a glass window. The nurses' station I presumed. I went and looked in the window, but no one was there. Inside I saw a blackboard, Room 1 Ferry, Amos; Room 2 Garner, Josephine; Room

3 Kama, Bane . I peeked around the corner and saw a short hallway with three rooms on each side.

I tiptoed down the hallway past Room One, then past Room Two, and stopped before Room Three. Banes door was open halfway. I wasn't sure if he was sleeping, so I quietly peeked in. He was wide-awake, with a woman straddling him in his bed and locked at his lips. Slowly I shuffled backed out of the room, my eyes clenched shut until I was in the hallway. That was no mouth-to-mouth resuscitation. Who the hell was that? I leaned against the wall to prevent myself from passing out.

"Help me! Somebody help me, I need help!" came from where the nurses' desk was.

A nurse plowed through a set of double doors at the end of the hall toward the screams. "Nettie, what you making a fuss about!"

"My grandbaby, she need help. That baby is coming, but I think it's stuck!"

"We can't help you right now, Nettie," the nurse said as she went back towards the double doors. "The doctor got a diver in here with a bad case of the bends. You gotta get your granddaughter over here." The nurse disappeared leaving the double doors swinging behind her.

Nettie went after her, but stopped at the doors. She turned around, her face soaked in sweat once again. I was the only one there, standing alone in the hallway.

She gave me a look like her day couldn't possibly get any worse.

"I'm a nurse, can I help you?" I said softly.

"You a nurse! What you standin' there for! Follow me!"

I followed Nettie's command and we ran down the dry, dusty road. I could have run faster but that wouldn't have done me any good because I didn't know where I was going. When we finally reached Nettie's shanty, she held on to the wooden gate in front, pushed it open and waved me in, trying to catch her breath. "You …you, go on in!"

I went through the gate, leaving Nettie bent over. I only got halfway to the door before I heard a scream that would make the earth shake. I quickened my step and went inside.

The kitchen was small, simple. I didn't see anyone so I ventured in further until I found Nettie's granddaughter lying in a bed soaking wet. Her gray cotton skirt was pulled up around her chest and she was bare below that.

"OOOOuuuuu!!!" she hollered again as if she were being gored. She pulled a pillow up close to her chest.

"It's OK, I'm a nurse, I'm here to help you," I tried to assure her. Oh, God, what do I do? I rotated through maternity in nursing school, but it was just a couple of days. When it was my turn to watch a live birth, I got paired with a single mother. She needed someone to hold her hand so I stood with her and cheered her on from the head of the bed. I didn't get to see anything until it was all over.

Water, boil water, towels, didn't they always call for towels? "Nettie! We need boiling water and towels!" I yelled towards the kitchen hoping she was there by now.

"OOOOOuuuu!!!" Nettie's granddaughter screeched again, louder if you could believe it.

The contractions must be getting closer, I thought to myself. I looked down, between her legs and saw a tiny foot popping out of her vagina. As the contractions clamped down, the foot became a leg, but that was all that was coming out.

The baby must be breached. "OK, I'll be right back."

I said to my patient as I ran in the kitchen to wash my hands and see about Nettie getting our supplies. When I got back into the kitchen, screaming Nettie's name, Nettie was by the back door, lying flat on the ground.

"Nettie," I screamed in fear myself. I pushed through the door that her body was half blocking and kneeled down beside her. She was as still as a lazy tourist. "Nettie!" I screamed again, this time shaking her. She giggled like a jellyfish, but didn't move on her own. I reached down to feel her jugular, no pulse.

"OOOUUUU!!!" Even louder this time from inside.

I had to choose, in that split second, who I was going to try and help live.

I ran back inside and scrubbed my hands with the sliver of soap at the sink. I grabbed the dirty dishtowel, the only thing I could find and went back to my screaming patient.

"OK, Trina, right?" I asked as I squatted at the end of the bed.

"Yes!!! OOOOOUUUUUU!!!"

"Ok, Trina, this is going to be a little uncomfortable, but your baby is trying to come out the wrong way. I am going to have to reach inside and try to turn the baby."

Trina didn't answer, she just moaned in horror. I prayed that she wouldn't die too on me. I took the baby's soft tiny foot and gently pushed it back in to its mother. Then, as gently as I could, I reached inside of Trina and felt my way around. When I felt the baby's chest, I firmly began to rotate the body so the head would face down. I tuned out Trina's pleas to stop. There was only one way she and this baby were going to stay alive, the baby had to come out, head first.

When the baby was in its proper position, I withdrew my bloody hand. With the next contraction the entire head slid through, then the shoulders and I helped it out from there. Trina was silent and I could only hope she wasn't in shock. I wrapped the baby, a little girl, in the dirty dishcloth. I pulled out the ribbon that tied my hair back and tied it around the umbilical cord; the baby shrieked.

"Oh, good Lord!" I heard from the kitchen. I turned and saw the nurse from the hospital. Behind her was a man, a doctor I hoped. The nurse took the baby from me and the man shook Trina until she whispered, "What is it?"

Chapter 47

JILL

JANUARY 3, 1996

I skipped breakfast and wandered down to the beach with my mother's journal and plopped myself down on the sand. The bay was as smooth as an ice rink right after the Zamboni has swiped it clean. The palms stood as still as my fellow vacationers lying asleep in their rooms. A lone jogger briskly ran along the bay, his faithful furry companion trotting behind, with his tongue flopping.

My mind volleyed back and forth like a tennis ball over a net. If, or should I say when, I see Bane, what should I say, how should I react, I thought? How could you! Hug him and say I'm so glad that you are OK! Kick him in the groin, how dare you use me! Be nonchalant, after all, I never asked him if he was seeing anyone else.

Before my cerebral wires shorted out, Bane came up from behind me, in his characteristic style with that trademark smile, saying "Hey!"

He leaned down to kiss me and I turned my cheek. He smelled unshowered and his hair was greasy. I never noticed that his legs were too short for his body. There were no fireworks igniting inside of me. He pulled back, tilted his head, but continued in his cheery tune, "Did you hear what happened?"

I looked at the ocean and drew in a deep breath. I

closed my mother's journal and held it tight to my chest, then looked up at him, my eyes squinting, "Bane, I know."

"It was unbelievable!" he started, clearly thinking I was talking about his adventure out at sea.

I interrupted him, "I saw you with that girl last night."

His face turned somber. He sat down in the sand next to me, wrapped his arms around his knees, and let his head fall forward until his chin rested on his chest.

"Listen," I continued. "I never asked you if you were involved with anyone else. On some level, I guess, I just wanted to let go, live in the moment, without a care in the world. But, that's really not my style; I'm a monogamous girl at heart. I'm not looking for a fling, I'm looking for someone who wants to share a life together."

Bane looked down at the sand and traced a pattern in the sand as I talked. Then he looked up and out at the sea. "I get that. She's a girl I know from a neighboring island. The dive community is pretty tight down here. When she got word of what happened, she came over to Triton."

"You don't have to explain yourself. There's a part of me that isn't sorry. I've had an amazing experience down here, much in part, thanks to you."

We sat in an awkward silence, not knowing where to go next. My anger now diffused, my mind clear. We are who we are, two very different people, whose worlds really don't match.

"When do you leave?"

"Later today."

"Did you want to do something this morning?"

I took another deep breath and thought briefly about that option. "Bane, I think it is probably best if we just say our goodbyes now."

He stood up slowly, swept the sand off himself, and extended a hand out to me. I put my mother's journal down on my chair and stood in front of him. I reached out my arms and wrapped them around his neck, slowly he reached around my waist and we held each other as he whispered, "I'm sorry."

"Don't be," I whispered back. "Thank you."

Chapter 48

JILL
JANUARY 4, 1996

"Thank God you're back!" Becky greeted me with a bear hug and pulled me into her apartment.

"I hope you don't mind me just showing up, I didn't know where else to go." I stood in her foyer feeling somewhat like a homeless person. Becky still had her scrubs on; she must have just got home from work. I, on the other hand, had a hot pink sweatshirt that said Triton on it with an image of the Triton shell and white sweatpants, my skin basted brown like my mother's Thanksgiving turkey.

"No, absolutely not, come in, I will make us some tea. I am so glad you're safe, we were all worried about you!" Becky grabbed my suitcase and stored it in her room. I met her in the kitchen and we sat at the kitchen table while we waited for steam to seep out of the kettle.

"Who's we?" I asked.

"Me, your brother and father, of course, and all the gals at work," Becky shared. "Marie wants to talk to you."

I looked into the teacup that had a lone green tea bag sitting at the bottom waiting to be warmed. It was time to face realty and make some decisions on how to proceed with my life. I know my escape only prolonged the inevitable, but at least now I felt strong enough to begin to move forward somehow.

"I'll call Marie tomorrow, see if I can set up a meeting with her."

"So, how was your trip?"

"I'm not even sure where to start," I began. For the next two hours I filled Becky in on all the details of my adventure. She listened earnestly like a child being read their favorite storybook and stopped to question or comment only during momentous parts of the tale.

"You actually snorkeled and looked over the wall? I could never do that!"

"Oh, my God, he disappeared, just disappeared into the ocean?"

"You could have been killed or kidnapped!"

And eventually, "Guys are dogs!" I know Becky wanted to make me feel better, and she was right that Bane did break my heart, but I didn't want to think of him like that.

Growling stomachs interrupted our conversation and we took a short break to order a pizza, Becky changed into sweats and we reconvened in the living room for a picnic on the couch.

By the time the ten o'clock news came on the TV, which we were not paying any attention to, we had a first draft of a plan on how to put my life back together. After a good nights sleep at Becky's, I would set out to conquer my first challenge. Meet with my brother, then father, and reestablish our relationship. It will not be the same, the little naive girl inside of me had died, morphed from a caterpillar to a butterfly, I guess. But, they were my family, and we needed to continue on together, even if it was different.

"Is one pillow enough?" Becky asked as she handed me one and dragged a queen size striped comforter behind her. I moved the couch pillows around to better accommodate a sleeping position.

"That will be great, thanks again, I really appreciate you letting me stay here tonight."

"No worries, you are welcome to stay as long as you like. The girls won't mind, they have friends come and go all the time. They are both working the night shift tonight, so we won't see them until morning."

"Sleep tight, everything is going to be OK," were Becky's last words as she flicked the light switch off and let me drift into a deep, dreamless sleep.

5 Years Later—2001

JILL

"Your husband is on the phone," Elaine whispered to me through the crack in the door.

"Can you please tell him I will call him back in a few minutes?" I whispered back not wanting to wake the little guy who was nestled in my arms. Baby Jones squirmed with the interruption. I hated to have to put him back in his bassinet; he had been screeching since my shift began at 4 o'clock, like most babies born to moms addicted to crack. It took me hours to get him to suckle his bottle, burp, bathe and change him. All the warmth and attention finally wore him out and he fell asleep.

I knew why Luke was calling. It was 7:30 and he always called so our girls could say goodnight. Then he would read them a story, just like I did, on the evenings I wasn't working. Little Samantha, who just turned two, would put up a good fight to stay awake like her sister two years ahead of her. She usually dozed off, however, before we even turned the first page.

Unlike Becky, I thought long and hard before I jumped into motherhood. Did I really want kids? If so, why? I overheard so many people my age say things like, "I really wasn't ready, but my mother wouldn't stop nagging me about wanting to be a grandmother" or "If I don't have kids, who will take care of me when I get old?" To each his own. For a long time I searched for a good reason for me to have kids. I needed to be clear why I would make the sacrifices I felt would be needed to be a good mother.

This maternity unit gave me the purpose my mind, heart and soul needed to enter motherhood myself. Helping Trina deliver her breached baby made me want to help more babies. Watching all these fresh, unique souls come in to the world, each with their own aura, and look in their eye, began to lessen the pressure of what I envisioned being a mother would be like. I began to believe that these bundles of cuteness came preloaded with their mission in life, their own unique skill set and when you spend time with a little tyke like Luther over there, you can't help but wonder if he hasn't cycled through this life thing more than a few times.

Luther came into this world a hefty 9 pounds, 4 ounces. His manila colored skin, and tight black curls, were a neutral palette against his gray, blue eyes. If you stopped to stare into them, as I liked to when he sat in my arms, swaddled in a soft white cotton receiving blanket, you got to know him. We would gaze into each other's eyes, me in wonder, he in knowing. While most newborns cannot properly focus their gaze, Luther had long moments when he could. His eyes seem to say, "Yeah, I know you, I've seen you around. I know your story. Yup, I'm here again, got things to do."

As softly as I could, I lay little Baby Jones down amongst his peers. We nearly had a full house tonight. Clara cooed in the corner of the nursery, while all the other babies' eyes were shut closed as they purred like kittens. It was during these rare quiet moments that I marveled at all the possibility in the room. Would one of these little ones grow up to discover a cure for cancer, beat Michael Jordan's record, or maybe become the first woman President of the United States?

It was Becky who had suggested that I consider working in maternity after she heard about my escapade on Triton Island. I still think about Trina and her little girl and wonder how they're doing. The nurse from Triton hospital sent me a letter as she promised soon after I arrived home. Trina and her daughter were doing well. Her aunt and uncle who lived on a neighboring island took them into their home. Her uncle was a revered pastor, so there was promise that Trina would finally have a healthy home. I only wish we could have saved Nettie. I never returned to the island but I hold the many memories of it dear to my heart.

Marie took it really hard when I announced that I would not be returning to my old job. "What do you mean, you're not coming back!" she said trying to hold her voice down. "Do you know how hard I lobbied to get your job back? You will only be on probation for one year!"

"I'm sorry, Marie. I really do appreciate how much you have helped me, and all the support, but I need a change. I need to start fresh." I tried to explain.

It was Dr. Sol who suggested that I apply here, to Rockland County Medical Center, and start anew. She put a good word in with the mother-baby nurse manager for me. Dr. Sol turned out to be more than a doctor to me. She really became an ally these past few years. Some may say she crossed some patient-client barriers while others would call it professional courtesy. Without a mother, I really appreciated having an older female confidant. After my experience with Trina and Samantha, the name they gave the baby from the accident, I am extremely grateful that I made it to adulthood before I lost my mother. Dr. Sol knew Samantha's pediatrician. Every now and then she would sneak me an update on how she was doing. The latest news was that the sister who adopted Samantha was engaged. They would be moving to New Jersey after the wedding this summer. They never did follow through with their threat to file a civil suit.

I wish Becky lived closer. She really hit it off with Jim and ended up getting married after dating him for a year. They both agreed they wanted to return down south to be closer to their families and start one of their own. We meet every summer on the Outer Banks in a big house right on the beach. It's always a fun time. Becky is almost finished with her degree to become a geriatric nurse practitioner. She always had a special way with the elderly.

Things just seemed to fall into place once I arrived back to New York from Triton island five years ago. At first, I stayed with my brother. I worked things out with both him and my dad. It was a little easier to do since my father had already broken up with Miss Silky Pajamas before I got home. He realized that he should have allowed himself more time to properly grieve before getting involved in a new relationship. That only lasted a few months though. At least Billy and I liked his next girlfriend who now is his wife.

I ran into Luke, a guy I went to high school with, at the deli one morning.

"How are you, Jill?" he asked shyly. "You look tan."

I knew, but didn't really know, Luke from high school. He was one of the tallest, burliest guys in our class. Most of us wondered why he wasn't on the football team rather than playing tuba in the band.

"Um, I hear you and Jack broke up," he added. "Would you like to go to a movie or something?"

I can't say I saw fireworks or felt a lightning bolt at that first re-encounter. I did, however, accept his invitation for a date. He grew on me like a Triton sunrise; just a little glow at first, but eventually a full, hot, bright and sunny day. And like the sun, he was dependable.

"Hi Babe, are you all getting ready for bed?" I asked when Luke answered the phone.

"Amanda insisted on wearing her favorite pink pajamas. I had to dig them out of the laundry," Luke said somewhat exasperated.

I laughed, "Let me talk to her."

"Hi, Mommy."

"Hi, baby. Daddy tells me you didn't want to wear the nice yellow pajamas I left out for you." As small as they were, they already knew their father had a soft heart.

"No, Mommy, I like the pink ones!"

"OK, but tomorrow, when Mommy tucks you in, you are going to wear the yellow ones so we can wash the pink ones."

"OK, Mommy."

"Good night, sweetheart, please put your sister on the phone." I waited while they made the exchange. "Hi, Sarah, what book are you reading tonight?"

"The one with the baby farm animals," she said excitedly. This was one of their favorites. Luke and I agreed that we would expose our children to as much nature and outdoors as possible. We loved taking a ride upstate on the weekends to visit farms and go camping.

"Well, you enjoy your story. I love you. Don't forget to brush your teeth and wash your face. Make sure Wilbur gets his face cleaned too." Wilbur was our first 'baby'. He was a chubby English bulldog with wrinkles in his face and polka dotty ears as the girls would say. Like a little kid, we had to wash his face, too, before he goes to bed.

"Love you too" Sarah said as her voice faded while she handed the phone back to Luke.

Although the girls could be a handful, I knew they loved their three nights a week alone with their dad while I worked. He loved the quality time too. I was so blessed to have a husband who supported all of me.

I still think of my mom every day. On my desk at home I keep a picture of me as a newborn in her arms. I wonder what she what she was thinking as she looks lovingly at me bundled up in her arms. I still have lots of questions to ask her. Many times I do. I talk to her out loud when I am alone, "Do you think Sarah is ready for a big girl bed?" "What should I make for dinner tonight?" "Would Luke prefer a blue or a red handmade knit sweater for Christmas this year?" She doesn't answer, but that's OK, because I know she's there.

About the Author

Sue Allison-Dean is a nurse who retired from traditional practice in 1999, after working 13 years as a Wound, Ostomy, Continence Clinical Nurse Specialist. She found a second career in gardening after working in a garden center and completing an organic gardening internship at Highgrove Garden in England. She now co-owns Naturescapes with her landscape designer husband, Robert. She has authored several clinical and horticulture articles and was a contributing author to the bestselling book, Touched By A Nurse. She is passionate about the sea and loves exploring tropical islands. She extends this passion by doing volunteer work benefitting dolphins and whales. Sue splits her time between Armonk, New York and Cary, North Carolina, with her husband and English bulldog, Bubba.

A Final Note

Dear Reader,

Thank you for reading *I Know You're There*. Honest reviews on Amazon, Barnes and Noble and Goodreads, as well as any social media platforms that you use, are greatly appreciated.

Contact information may be found on my website, www.susanallisondean.com .

Let's connect:
Twitter: @sueallisondean
Facebook: https://www.facebook.com/pages/Susan-Allison-Dean/388024291305521